The Northlore Series
Volume One
Folklore

NORDLAND

www.nordlandpublishing.com

Dedication

To those who dream of Ice and Snow.

Contents

Introduction

The word *folk-lore* first appeared in print in 1846, yet the concept it encompassed was far from new. Storytelling is probably as old as humankind itself, and the fables that cultures develop and transmit down through the ages reveal much of what they once thought and believed. This is certainly true of the northern peoples, whose stories reveal a fascination with what today we would term, *paranormal phenomena*. If the ancient forebears of modern Scandinavia believed in anything, it was unseen spirits, creatures of the forest, and things that went bump in the night.

The Scandinavian peoples came originally from a world of mists and forests, a landscape that spawned a rich history of myth and legend, which entered the collective psyche and formed the bedrock of their soul. Although severely diminished by the arrival of Christianity in the last millennium, these beliefs never fully died out. Many have been preserved as fragments in songs and sagas, while others survive as stories, still told by parents to their children.

Needless to say, these tales were far from being merely entertainment. They had a valid and often chilling message relevant for a pagan people. At the root of the stories, there are lessons to be a learned; little nuggets of wisdom that made sense in their time, and perhaps still makes sense today.

This collection owes itself to inspiration from these ancient tales, retold now in new and sometimes surprising ways. Through humour, adventure and nightmarish horror, we find Trolls in caves, Huldr in forests, Witches and Selkies and mischievous Elves far closer to home than you might ever wish. Welcome to the Northlore series. Warning: do *not* feed the animals.

MJ Kobernus, Norway 2015

Hold the Door

Sarah Lyn Eaton

"Holda! Away from the door!" My mother's words were thick with fear. I frowned at my work. Delicate drafts nipped at my fingers where they pressed the cob mixture of sand, clay, and straw into the cracks around the doorway. The temporary patches were already freezing against the storm outside, but they helped in our battle against the winter wights attempting to reclaim our space. And it kept me occupied while we waited.

After three weeks away at hunt, the men of our village were still lost in the storm that had crept in after their departure, my father amongst them. I pulled the wool plug from a small hole in the door and spied outside. The combination of howling wind and swirling snow blurred the landscape beneath thick, fat flakes.

"Away from the door!" My mother barked a second command.

"Do you not hear your mother's voice? A shadow moves across our threshold!" My grandmother chastised me. "The forest trolls cloak themselves in such storms. Do you not listen to the winter tales?"

I stood up, unsure. My mother and bestemor kept close to the lit hearth, their eyes on the wall behind me. My smaller brothers, wrapped in reindeer hides for warmth, sat near their feet. Gylfi's eyes were wide with fear. He was young enough that the tales of forest trolls were a source of his nightmares. Ríki's older eyes dreamed of battling the invaders.

The fire flared dully behind them in its own battle against the winter air that seeped in where the smoke escaped through the roof. I turned back to scrape the cob from my hand into the bucket as something large thundered past the outside wall. I froze.

"Holda! Away to me!" My mother commanded again. I stumbled backwards as something heavy threw itself against our oaken door, a prized wood foraged from neighboring lands. I could hear the snuffling grunt of a large predator and the long slow scraping of nails against wood.

"Is it a troll?" Gylfi trembled.

"It doesn't smell of troll," Ríki whispered. "And it's daylight."

"The sun has not been able to penetrate the snow clouds for weeks," Heimlaug shook her head, turning to my mother. "Your children lack common sense."

"Is it father?" Gylfi asked hopefully. My grandmother snorted at him.

"Your father would use words instead of claws."

"Trolls don't have claws," Ríki's voice was disappointed.

"What if father was frozen?" I asked. The men had been gone for longer turns at hunt, but never in such weather. My question seemed to give the other women pause and I took the moment to creep back to the door. I put a hand to it just as the weight fell against it again. I could feel the heat of it and quickly snuck a look. "It's a bear!" I sighed, slightly less fearful.

My mother cried out. She wrapped her animal skin tightly around her torso, pressing herself fearfully into the wall. It was unnerving. My mother was the one who spun tales of the forest trolls, mountain dwarves, and river elves over the evening fires. She was the one who left offerings for the nisse who tended our lands while we slept. A fire flooded through my veins at the sight of her fear.

"Can we kill it?" I asked, my stomach rumbling.

"We cannot kill a prowling animal while hiding inside the cave," grandmother Heimlaug said, her heavily-ringed hand resting on the knife that she wore. The blade had belonged to grandfather Bergsveinn, second to the Jarl of the village. Grandfather had gone out to sea on a raid one summer and had not returned. When she was lost in thought, grandmother's head was always facing the direction of the sea. This time the men had gone inland, but in her worry, my grandmother's eyes turned to the wintry waters in the bay.

"What color is its pelt?" My mother's words formed crystals as the air around her suddenly chilled.

I took a breath and put my eye again to the unplugged hole. A black nose pressed itself immediately to the hole, snuffling at the scent of me. Its breath was hot and not unwelcoming in the cold. But death waited in its giant jaws. It turned its head.

"White." I stared in disbelief, having never seen a bear from the far North within the boundaries of our village.

"Does it want to eat us?" Ríki asked.

"Yes," grandmother said. "Some more than others." She ruffled his hair.

"Holda," my mother whimpered at me.

"Alfrún," my grandmother said, her voice grinding above the battering at the door, "be my son's wife and stand your ground."

"I was something else before I was his wife," my mother shifted in her discomfort.

"We do not look backwards. We go forward. It is our way."

"The legends and histories woven nightly in the Great Hall contradict you." Beneath their hard words, I heard a bit of my mother come back to her voice.

"The bear will move on, mother," I comforted. "Our door is strong and there are other halls in the village to try." My little brother was standing at my hip, a small axe in his hand.

"Can I see it?" Gylfi asked. He had never seen a bear that was not a pelt on the bed. I pulled a low grain barrel towards the door and helped him clamber on top of it, level with the hole. He recoiled momentarily at the blast of cold, and I watched as his eyes went wide and quiet. "It's laying down."

"Barricade the door," my mother whispered.

* * * *

Grandmother was watchful. Mother was worried. I grabbed for the heavy plank by the door. Ríki leapt up and helped Gylfi grapple with the other end. Together, the three of us slid it across the entranceway. The worry lines around my mother's wider, grey eyes softened. Her dark complexion, where my father, grandmother, and the others of our village were fair, sang its own tale of her foreign birth.

According to grandmother Heimlaug's stories, my father was just a young man when he brought my mother back from a raid. Father publicly doted and lavished jewels on her, but it was obvious to all that she was the greater treasure. She wore each trinket he gifted her with for only one evening, after which she placed it in a small wooden chest, candlelight glinting off the other precious metals and gems tucked inside.

I asked her once why she did not wear the tribute from father. Her reply was simple. "Every jewel is a plea for my heart, a gift I give freely."

The village had eaten well of fish since her arrival, for she ventured out to sea with the fishermen, standing at the prow, steering them to where the schools lay in rest. She was beloved. Yet, in the Great Hall, over cups of mead, of boasts and brags, no one told of her origin. She was half-stranger still, though she was not strange to me. For the elders, she was an outsider. For me and my brothers, she had always been a child of the fjord.

But she wasn't. Her moods were cold, as changeable as our sea. The only constant was her devotion to my father. His love, in turn, was a common boast in the Great Hall, his passion spilling out of his cup in sweeping tales of Odin's love for Frigg. Grandmother did not think it befitting of a man to be so besotted with a woman, especially the son of Bergsveinn. It was a discussion they had often, in the following morning, over bowls of savory porridge.

"She loves you as a woman who must love," grandmother would fret.

"I may not be her sun, but she is my moon, and she chooses me," he would smile. In further answer, my father would weave sober tales of the love his father had for his mother and my grandmother would quiet her words, excusing herself to go outside and search for ghosts among the waves of the sea. My mother would smile at him then, and we could see the great love in her heart grow stormy and wild.

In the darkness, when my parents joined together and we were meant to be sleeping, I heard him whisper fervently for her to melt to him. And in that darkness, when he pleaded softly to my mother, she whispered. "You have given me myself, and I stay. That is all the love that is mine to give."

Now my mother flared her nostrils in panic, looking to the shadows of our home for my father's strength. Grandmother clasped her hand, passing a look between them, and she stilled. My younger brother pressed his eye again to the door, one hand on the plank that barred it closed.

"It's gone," he said.

"Are you certain?" grandmother asked, drawing herself up from her chair.

"I can't see it," Gylfi shrugged. I motioned to Ríki and he helped us remove the barrier. I plucked Gylfi from his barrel, pushing it away, and pulled the door gently, the icy chill biting at my fingers. Winter licked at my face as I peered out. I saw no trace of the beast save for footprints at our door. Already the snow was sweeping them away.

"He's right," I reported, closing the door again.

"A hungry bear will not wander long from a laden pantry." Grandmother patted my mother's hand with no trace of ire as she assumed command. "We must warn the others to gather in the Great Hall. Best we stand together against the danger than be picked off one family at a time."

"I will run to the houses," I said. It only made sense. Amongst us, I was the quickest. "I will alert the families. And then I will get us safely to town."

"We can go to town on our own," Ríki puffed out his chest.

"You can, my little men," grandmother Heimlaug said kindly. "But your mother cannot. She needs all of our help."

"No." My mother shook her dark braids. "I will stay. I will wait here. You must all go."

"Nonsense," my grandmother dismissed. "What good would it do for my son to come home if I have lost him his wife?" Grandmother removed grandfather's blade from her belt and crossed the small room, handing it to me. The carved bone handle was heavy. I could feel the age of it against my flesh. "My husband's sword may have fallen with him on foreign lands but this blade never failed him." Her rough skin held mine firmly, the metal tooth between us. Her eyes were bright and clear. As she looked at me, I saw the ghosts of all those she had sent to danger. My father had once had brothers. "If you have need of it, may Bergsveinn's blade find its mark. May you cut well."

I tied the sheath to my belt as Ríki handed me woolen fleecing to pad the inside of my boots. My mother wrapped our thickest fur around my shoulders and pulled the hood up. Her eyes betrayed her fear for me but her tongue would not allow it purchase. She was Alfrún, the wife of Heimkell, the son of Heimlaug, the daughter of Haukr the Hammer.

I kissed my brothers and stepped out quickly into the elements. The boys slammed the heavy door shut behind me. The snow wights stripped breath from the air mercilessly and my chest tightened painfully. I inhaled lightly, the heat of my exhalations stoking a fire against the crisp chill clawing its way inside. My eyes opened wide now that I was outside the smoky interior, but the world around me whirled a dusky white in the absence of sunlight.

I made for the next home, just over the ridge. In the swirling snow, I was quick to imagine lumbering beasts everywhere. I could hear nothing over the roaring wind, not even the surf that crashed against the ice at the shoreline. Despite the wind, I was sure-footed in the storm. Even half-blind, the way would have been easy for any grown child of our village.

When I was small, my father would blindfold me at dusk, spin me around in the farmlands, and slap my bottom hard, bidding me to head for home. I believed my father was right beside me. I believed that he was watching over me. Each time I journeyed unsighted, I believed I was safe.

One day I fell off a low cliff and broke my arm. I sat quietly on a jagged rock, biting my lip against the pain, waiting for my father to scoop me up into his thick arms. I sat still for perhaps an hour, waiting, until I finally removed my blindfold and saw that I was alone.

I made my way home, clutching my broken arm to my side. I did not cry when it was bound tightly to heal. I did not cry the next time I was left in the field with no sight. I listened to the whispers of the land wights. I learned their wind songs. I learned the way. All the children did. We learned the way to every home.

Smoke piping out from the roof of the next dwelling proved my feet true. I banged on the door until Sefa unplugged the small sight hole. The bright blue of her eye peered at the little of my face visible beneath the hood.

"Holda?"

"A bear from the North attacked our home! Heimlaug bids everyone to the Great Hall!" Sefa's eye grew wide and she nodded. I did not wait, but moved quickly on, zig-zagging from family to family with my warning.

By the time I reached the center of the village, my muscles were stiff with cold. After knocking on his door, Lame Lófi stood me beside his forge fire to thaw. Pulling a hat on over his unkempt red hair, he left to reach those closest to the Great Hall, where smoke billowing from the roof was a welcome sign to the heavily-furred bundles already making their way inside.

As soon as my limbs warmed enough to be limber, I left the blacksmith's workshop. Ours was the furthest home at the edge of the village against the sea. I ran a straight path back to fetch my family, fleet-footed, my earlier prints already lost beneath drifting snow.

A scream greeted me at the rise of the hill. Was it Gylfi? Ríki? The white bear stood on his hind legs, dwarfing our small home. I foolishly realized it had most likely never left.

I stumbled as the great bear slashed downwards, breaking the heavy door beneath its rage. The earth trembled beneath me as the bulk of its giant body slammed into the ground. I unsheathed grandfather Bergsveinn's blade with a cry of my own. The bear turned its giant head towards me. We became two mighty creatures running at each other. I could feel the force of his charge quaking the air before me. I slid on ice, falling as he flew over me. I lashed out with my metal tooth and was rewarded with drops of warm, rich blood on my face. The bear howled and hobbled away, into the storm.

"Holda!" My mother stood in the broken doorway, holding my brothers firmly behind her. Fear, fury, and worry battled across her face, as she glanced from where I lay on the snow to where the bear had disappeared into the storm. I pushed myself to my feet, bloody blade in hand and went to them, my heart thumping in my chest.

"You took on the bear!" Gylfi exclaimed.

"Your father will be proud of you, granddaughter." Heimlaug's blue eyes glinted with relief at my return.

"Only if we are alive to greet him," I shook my head at the ice crystals infiltrating our home. The door lay broken in three large pieces and a myriad of splinters. "We cannot stay here now."

We bundled up beneath all of our furs and hides. Grandmother covered the stew pot and pulled it off the fire with a square of leather. I reached out a hand to take it from her but she slapped me away, pointing at the weapon I carried. I would take point. Ríki grabbed the other side of the pot to help her carry it. Gylfi clutched his small axe in one hand and my mother's hand with his other.

I took the shortest path to the village, eyes sweeping left and right, blade unsheathed. My mother held to my fur from behind, while my grandmother and Ríki lagged at the rear with the stew pot. I stopped, trying to yell back at them above the roar of the storm. I was worried at their distance. Grandmother shook her head and waved at me dismissively. I nodded. Heimlaug, daughter of Haukr was not yet ready to leave the walking world.

Lame Lófi was waiting at the entrance of the Great Hall, his red hair blistered with ice where it hung below his hat. He smiled, hurrying to open the doors, always favoring his right leg. The heat from within lashed at my cheeks. The wife of Jarl Rúnólfr, Lady Olaug met us at the door, her white hair thickly braided. She held her hands out to take mine, warmly. Lófi started at the sight of the bloody blade in my fist. He glanced over our party.

"Is everyone all right?" he asked.

"Nothing I couldn't handle." I nodded, embarrassed to have waved the bloody weapon at Lady Olaug. I wiped it off on the edge of my tunic before sheathing it. My hands were shaking.

"You are the reason we are all safe," Olaug smiled, pulling me to the blazing fire as my mother removed my furs. I could feel life returning to my limbs, my face hot with biting frost. Sefa handed us each a hot cup of broth.

"Holda's blade bit into the flesh of the great bear!" Ríki exclaimed, drawing attention to our arrival.

"It is my grandfather's blade," I mumbled hotly.

"Not any longer, granddaughter." Heimlaug turned from setting her pot at the edge of the hearth. "Were he alive he'd gift it to you himself."

"My husband shall hear of this, little shield maiden," Olaug noted. She hugged my grandmother tightly and turned to survey the room.

We found ourselves a dry spot against the wall near the fire, and made a nest with our furs. My mother was softer now, comforted by the noise of people around her. What panic had gripped her, trapped in our home, began to ebb. She smiled at me as I tucked her hide around her core.

"You did well, Holda. Your father would hardly have done better," she stroked my cheek and I blushed.

"Do not heap too much praise on her," my grandmother teased gruffly, "lest she think herself invincible."

"Save some bears for me, Holda!" Ríki puffed out his chest again, posturing.

"Rawr!" Gylfi jumped out at him and my brothers ran off to play with the other young children in a corner away from the door. My grandmother stared at me.

"You have the look of your mother, but the eyes of your grandfather peer from your face. Your father's courage flows through you." What I felt was exhaustion. Grandmother touched my chin with her knuckles. "What did you think when you charged the great bear?"

"I did not think, grandmother. If I had, I might not have begun to run." She chuckled brightly at my honesty.

"Attend to our people with the Lady Olaug, Holda. She is my dearest friend. I will stay with your mother."

The Jarl's wife was in a far corner, tending to a man. He shuddered beneath a matted pelt. I ran to them. The Lady smiled grimly as I bent beside her.

"It seems our guest had cause to best your beast as well."

"Has he come from our men? Does he know how their hunt fares?"

"I am afraid he has wandered in on our misfortunes, having lost his way in the storm."

"He is injured," I saw blood beneath his pelt. His eyes flickered at me, nostrils flaring to take in my scent. I felt the heat of his exhalation and the hair on my neck rose.

"Half-blood," he threw his head back and laughed, bearing his teeth. "And I thought this winter would be a lean one. Instead, I feast."

I ripped the pelt away, revealing a ragged cut running up his torso. Cold flooded through me as a prickling heat grew in its wake. I drew my blade once more.

"Holda!" Lady Olaug exclaimed, reaching for my arm. The stranger began to laugh and rise, to shake and growl as his skin split. The animal beneath revealed itself. The villagers in the hall began to run from him. The giant snow beast stood, blood seeping gently from his belly. He towered above me, new bones snapping into place.

"Shifter," the women hissed, drawing blades. Everywhere, metal teeth glinted in the firelight. The great bear's eyes fixated on my mother, who paled behind me. She backed away from our nest towards the door. The bear stalked forward and I kept pace between them.

"Hold the door, Holda," my mother said softly. I felt the storm hit me from behind as others gasped at the sudden chill. The fires blanched in the hearth.

"Mother, no," I begged.

"I stayed for your father," she said, wrapping her hide tighter around her core. "And I leave for you."

When she ran, the bear roared and reared. I screamed and plunged my arms up as high as I could, ramming my blade into its heart. His mighty claw swiped at my arm, nails scraping along bone. I heard the cracking sound but could not register what it meant. The bear staggered out of the Great Hall and I followed, my blade deep in its skin.

Others called out after me in protest as the Great Hall doors closed behind me. The trail of blood weeping down my weakened arm began to freeze, giving me respite from the pain. The bear and I ran after the same dark shape. My mother turned at the edge of the ice flow and stared at me, her eyes large and dark. The hide around her torso began to shrink and stretch and reshape itself until she bobbed out across the ice, her flippers slapping ungracefully on the frozen land. I stared, mouth open in confusion and wonder. Her eyes stared at me still, but they wore a new face. The bear caught her scent and lumbered towards her.

"Alfrún!" A voice thundered over the sounding storm from the top of the hill. My father had returned! I watched, spellbound, as he ran for the water. The other men from our village followed him up over the rise. There were not as many men as when they left us, but those that remained fell upon the slowing bear with swords and axes. With a vengeful fervor, they took his head. But my father kept running, slipping across the ice. I made for the shore.

"Father!" He looked at me with tired eyes, but his attention was focused on the sea water. A pale head swam beneath the waves and we watched together. I fell beside him, the sudden weight of me distracting his heart.

"Holda, you are bleeding." I could hardly feel his eyes on me. His beard was encased in ice crystals and his face bore spots bitten by frost. But his eyes were brilliantly blue. I started to lose myself to the cold of them. My teeth drummed so loudly I was sure they would crack. The ice shifted beneath us.

"Our daughter's wound needs tending." My mother's voice was a fire in my blood. My father turned in surprise, but the mere nearness of her set him right. He ripped a length of my tunic hem and began to wrap it around my arm tightly. Only then did I feel the pain in the bone. The same arm I had broken in my youth. I watched my parents, like children, touching each other as if for the first time.

"You left." The agony in father's voice was heartbreaking. My mother wrapped her hands in his beard and pressed her forehead to his.

"Not today. But that day will still come."

"I hope I do not live to see it," he smiled and kissed her. My mother looked at me. I reached out and touched her hide, clutched tightly to her side. She took my hand in hers and kissed the palm of it, tears in her eyes.

"This is Bergsveinn's blade," a voice exclaimed. I looked up as the elderly Jarl pulled it from the carcass. "Who wielded this blade? This is the kill that felled the beast. This is the hand that has fed our people and avenged our men."

My father looked on in surprise as my mother pushed me forward. I rose wobbly to my feet. "I did, Jarl Rúnólfr." The old man's eyes twinkled in wonder.

"We have hunted this creature for weeks. He killed three of our men. He seemed to be running from us but I fear we were fools. He led us the furthest from our home we have been in winter, and then he doubled-back." The Jarl smiled incredulously. "And fell against a daughter of our village. We will leave the liver to our gods. The heart belongs to you, Holda, daughter of Heimkell and Alfrún."

I stood tall as my father tucked me beneath his cloak. "I stabbed the great bear in defense of my mother."

"Ahh, your mother. A rare treasure she is, to all of us." No one else seemed surprised that my mother was soaking wet in the wintry air with little effect. "Have you ever heard the story of how Alfrún came to find your father in the ocean, clinging to a broken prow of a ship? We had thought Heimkell lost, until she brought him back to us."

"I have never heard that story."

"There is room in all tales of love for magic," Jarl Rúnólfr smiled. He held my blade out and I stepped forward to take it, leaving my parents to each other. He took my shoulder in his hand as he would one of his warriors. "You have spilled blood in defense of our people and we will hear of your battle. But let there be warmth and mead among our tales tonight, for we have long been away from our fires and our families!" The tired men roared in agreement making for the hall with renewed vigor.

Behind us, the great bear bled red into the snow. The richness of magic in the shifter's blood sated the angry winter wights. As the doors of the Great Hall opened, the storming snows around us stilled.

Mara, my love

On the forest fringe shadows grow long.
Barred wooden shutters deny the call.
Our fingers clasped together, locked,
an indurate mutuality of flesh, of bone.
Her silent lips refuse to name the hour,
now rising in those conquered eyes.
She kisses my hand, and strokes my cheek,
disrobes and reveals her shapely form.
And still, unbidden, the coils of lust
stir as she walks out into the cold
without one last glance, or feeling flinch.
Yet I do not follow with shawl in hand,
to drape across those shoulders bare.
But bolt the door, slammed hard behind,
with a fistful of iron and eyes tightly closed.
Thoughts of my love, that tender soul,
framed by a sudden, monstrous howl.

By Andrew James Murray

The Journal

MJ Kobernus

Some stories don't make sense, full of sound and fury, signifying nothing. And maybe this journal is just that; a tale told by an idiot. You must judge for yourself, but I assure you that the events portrayed here are accurate. I put together the pieces myself, and it's all true. That's my job: I'm a reporter.

It all began with a missing girl. I was on my way to the courthouse in Hamar to report on a possible abduction or murder. This confusion on the part of the Crown was unusual. There was no body, no evidence and yet they were trying for a prosecution. I remember thinking how amazed I would be if this didn't get thrown out.

I was hurtling north on E6 and was soon in cowland, the urban sprawl of Oslo left far behind. I didn't really mind a jaunt into the countryside, but it never paid to let your editor know that. Better to let him think I was doing him a big favour, schlepping all the way out to the sticks. Besides, I didn't like the way he dumped the assignment on me last minute.

I was in the shower when the phone rang. Ain't that always the way of it? I took my time answering, but I was still dripping when I got to my mobile. I wiped my hands on the towel I had thrown around my waist, then picked up the phone.

"Yeah?"

"Eirik. About bloody Goddamn time. I have an assignment for you."

"Who is this?" I could not help teasing. Bjorn Asgeir was notoriously short tempered. He was a big man with a mop of shaggy hair, and I enjoyed poking the bear, as I called him, whenever I could.

"Stop messing around. You want it or not?"

I didn't have anything much to do right then. I'd just finished a piece exposing corruption in contract placements in one of the larger counties, but now I was at a loose end. "Sure. What you got?"

He cleared his throat. "That business of the missing farm girl is going to court today to determine if there is a case to answer."

I had read something a couple of weeks back, but my memory ain't what it once was. That half-empty bottle of Smirnoff on the kitchen table might have something to do with it.

"I'm gonna need a little more than that." I could imagine Bjorn getting red and I swear I could hear his teeth grinding.

"Goddammit, Eirik. You follow the news, don't you? Faen, you should. Old man. Farm. Beautiful girl. Presumed dead?"

It all came back to me. Yes. The old man that lived on an isolated farm with his daughter. She had simply vanished. The farmer had not reported her missing, so suspicion had naturally fallen on him. And the fact that a nationwide appeal had not turned up a single sighting of her gave some weight to the notion of foul play.

"Oh, you mean the Isaak Fetun case."

"That's it." Bjorn sounded slightly mollified. I'd probably needled him enough for the time being, so I decided to play at being a conscientious employee. Just to see how it felt.

"Sure, I know it. You want me to cover the trial. No problem"

"It's in Hamar, so you'll need to get your skates on."

"Hamar? That's a two hour drive! You couldn't have asked me last night?" Of course he couldn't. He was only asking me now because someone else had let him down. I didn't give a damn about that, but it was worth letting him know I was aggrieved, make him feel that he owed me one. I swore under my breath.

"Now, Eirik. You know I think highly of you. Get me the story and next time I'll give you more notice. Eight hundred words. And I want the copy on my desk first thing tomorrow."

"Alright, I'll do it."

Eight hundred words is a lot for a story like that. But I'm an old hand at this sort of thing. There'd be no need for me to rush home and burn the midnight oil. These days I could do the work anywhere and just email it. No one actually delivered typed up copy anymore. If I could, I would not even bother going to the office at all. Socialising with the other reporters held no interest. I could do more work from my desk than a dozen reporters in the bullpen. And no one would get on my case if I wanted to have a drink or two during the day. I made a mental note to fill my hip flask. It was going to be a long drive.

* * * *

The courthouse in Hamar was a reserved and unassuming place, with that ever-present smell of fresh floor wax. I almost fell on my ass as I hurried inside.

They seem to take a perverse delight in making wooden floors potential death traps. I asked one of the duty guards about it; a dour faced little man.

"You know why, don't you?" he said.

"No. Go on, tell me."

"It's to discourage the accused from making a break for it. They'd slip and break their neck before they were halfway to the door."

I smiled. Who knows, maybe there's some truth in it. What else could explain the almost pathological obsession with polishing?

"So which room is the Fetun case?"

"Courtroom six," he replied, pointing the way, but I was already moving. I knew the layout. After covering more than a dozen high profile cases here over the years, I should.

The session had already started, so I slipped inside and made my way to the gallery. I spotted the familiar faces of other journalists, and I doled out a nod in greeting where appropriate. For some, a cold stare through narrowed eyes was their lot. I got more than my fair share of snubs in return. Journalists can be a finicky bunch. We all hate each other really, but pretend friendship and camaraderie. Or perhaps that's just me?

I could easily make out Isaak Fetun. Sixty years old, but still a fit man. Farm work was hard, and only hard people did it. But he had the look of a drinker. He wore a blue suit and could have passed for one of the attorneys, except he was in the hot seat, reserved for the accused. When he looked around, I could see his mouth was a thin line, his brow furrowed. An angry pissed off drinker, maybe?

The prosecution began with an opening statement and I automatically jotted down notes. I steeled myself for the day ahead and wondered if I could take a nip from my flask without anyone noticing.

Things proceeded along the usual lines, but suddenly it got interesting when Fetun's lawyer, a man named Andersen, stood up.

"Your honour, my client wishes to know precisely what he is accused of. If it is murder, then where is the proof? Habeus corpus, your honour. They have yet to produce a body."

"I will kindly thank the council for the defence to not point out the obvious," retorted the judge. "The prosecution has argued convincingly that there is a case to answer. There is precedent. At the very least, she was abducted."

The accused shook his head, crossing his arms. He stared down at the floor. He appeared to say something, but it was too quiet to hear.

The judge thundered, "We will have the truth of it!"

At this Fetun leapt to his feet. "She's gone! She's gone and there's nothing anyone can do to bring her back."

Andersen tried to shush him, but it was too late. If that was not a confession, what was? The Crown prosecutors looked at each other smugly, the courtroom stirred with excitement, reporters busily tapping on their Blackberries, sending live updates.

"Settle down," yelled the judge, banging his gavel. "Mr. Fetun, are you telling us that you know what happened to your daughter?"

Isaak Fetun looked as if he regretted his outburst, but it was too late. He shook his head and sat, slumping in his seat like a man defeated. They could not get anything more out of him. The judge adjourned the session and we broke for lunch.

I went outside into the corridor, and decided to sneak a drink. I just needed to find a quiet spot. I tried one of the doors. There was a bathroom sign, pointing along the corridor. Perfect.

I managed to get inside the stall and get my flask out, but before I could take a nip, the door to the bathroom banged open.

"You have five minutes, Fetun."

The door slammed shut again, and I could hear footsteps approaching over the polished marble. The door to the stall next to mine opened and closed. Fetun was here? This was a golden opportunity. I started the record function on my phone.

"Hey buddy?" No reply. Funny how some people don't like to be bothered when they're using the can.

"Fetun," I whispered. "My name's Eirik. I'm a reporter. Give me a statement, and I can give you a shot of fifty percent proof. Interested?"

This got a response. "What do you mean?"

"You give me a statement, and I'll give you a pull of this flask."

I stood on the toilet seat rim, trying my damnedest not to fall in. I peered over the open top to the stall next door. Fetun was sitting on the throne but the lid was down. He had his head in his hands. When he looked up and saw the hip flask in my hand, his eyes lit up and he stared hungrily, biting his bottom lip. So, he *was* a drinker.

"Yeah, okay. What you want to know?"

I passed him the flask and he took a long pull, sighing with satisfaction. A little colour came back to his pallid face.

"First off, did you do it?"

"Like I would tell you if I did! But for the record, no. I did not kill my daughter."

"So where is she then? You know what happened to her, right?" He looked up at me then, his eyes slightly narrowed. He stared for a moment, then seemed to come to a decision.

"Yeah, I know what happened to her. She's not dead. She just went back."

"Went back where?"

"Where she came from of course. They come from the forest, and they go back to the forest."

I had no idea what he was talking about, but I pressed on. "So, if the police scour the area around your farm, they won't find her?"

He snorted. "Her kind don't get found, less they want to be found." He took another drink, then passed the flask back to me. I guess he could see a hungry look in my eyes too. I took a pull and felt the raw burning of the alcohol as it slid down my throat. When it hit my gut, it created a heatwave, permeating my body. I let out a sigh of deep satisfaction and passed back the flask. Fetun took a shallow sip.

"What do you mean, her kind?" I asked.

"You wouldn't believe me, if I told you, so just leave it. They don't like people prying into their business. If you know what's good for you, you'll forget I said anything."

He didn't know me. But it doesn't take a genius to figure out that I'm the kind of man that when you tell him not to do something, then you'd better stand back.

"Sure, sure," I said, placatingly. "You finish the flask. I have a feeling it'll be your last for a while."

He shrugged and knocked back the last of the vodka. The bathroom door opened and one of the guards entered. "That's it then Fetun, let's go."

Isaak Fetun pulled the flush and stood. He returned the flask, then whispered. "No matter what happens, just know this. She ain't dead, and I ain't no killer."

He opened the door to the stall and stalked out. He stopped to wash his hands, then I could hear him and the guards leave. I looked regretfully at the flask in my hand. It had paid for something. But what? One thing was for sure, I wasn't gonna let his warning put me off. I replayed a section of the interview. His voice was thin and reedy, but it was clearly him. *They don't like people prying into their business.* Just who were *they*? I had to find out.

* * * *

Fetun was remanded into custody. No going home for him. I wrote up my piece and sent it in, while sitting out in my car. I included part of the personal interview with yours truly, ending with, *whatever the outcome of the hearing, Isaak Fetun is winning no friends in court. His apparent attempt to lay the groundwork with an insanity plea did not deter the prosecution council and the Crown will pursue a charge of abduction.*

Fetun seemed like a smart, honest man. My gut told me he didn't do it, but it was clear he was hiding something. His story was incredible. They had badgered him, goading him into talking. And boy, did he talk! He told the court that an old woman had turned up at his door with a new-born babe in arms, telling him the kid was his. And he had reared the child, right up until she was eighteen when, according to Fetun, she had just walked into the forest and never come back. If there was a grain of truth to this, then why didn't he call child services when he was first given the baby? How could he possibly believe the kid was his? It was all quite ridiculous.

I decided to pay a visit to his farm at Hulderdal. It was only another hour's drive. I entered the address into the navigation system and was on my way. The route took me into the mountains. It seemed that his place really was remote. There were no more cars on the road, which quickly turned to gravel and then to mud. I wound my way up, surrounded by the thick green of virgin forest. No cutting was allowed here, not since the road was made. The trees were protected, and many of them were huge. Not quite like the Redwoods at Sequoia, but big by Norwegian standards.

When I got to the farm, it was ten after six. I was hungry, I needed a drink and I knew I was not likely to get either for a few more hours at least, so my mood was not the best. Still, I was there, and I wanted to have a look around; get a feel for the place. You can tell a lot about a man from how he lives.

It looked like any other working smallholding. A tractor, some heavy equipment that I did not recognise, barns, outbuildings and such. There was no cattle though. Where were his cows? Still, nothing strange, or unusual as far as I could see. I wandered around a bit, coming to the back of the barn. All I could see was a path leading into the brooding forest. My gut told me to check it out, so I followed it. My gut was right. Before I came to the border between field and forest, I found something not more than a few hundred meters from Fetun's farm.

A heavy canvas tarp covered a small mound. Flies buzzed madly around it. Even from a dozen paces, the smell was bad. I wrinkled my face and covered my nose and mouth with my hand, before edging closer. There was no way the police would have missed something so obvious, surely? As I got closer, the smell became more powerful, almost physical. I lifted the edge of the rough canvas with my foot, causing a cloud of flies to erupt into the air. Barely containing my disgust, I leaned over and heaved the canvas aside. I almost threw up then. I thought I was ready for anything, but I was wrong.

* * * *

Isaak Fetun knew that nothing he did or said would make any difference now. This was just how it was. He had known what he was getting into and, God forgive him, it had been worth it. That one night, and then all those years looking after her. His little Brighitta. But the old woman had warned him. *Not a soul, neither living nor dead, could know the truth of the matter*, and he had practically told that reporter everything, and the whole court! He could not keep his mouth shut. He got angry and the words just came out. He knew what he had to do. If he didn't it would be the worse for him.

Fetun stood slowly and removed the belt from around his waist. There, on the window, bars to stop him escaping. Well, they were wrong about that. He dragged the small chair over to the wall and stood on it. Passing the belt around the bar, he secured it into a loop. He stared at it for a moment and took a deep breath. He smiled as he realised how foolish that was, then he put his head through the leather noose. He settled it around his neck before hesitating, looking up at the ceiling. There was a sound like a chair falling over, then nothing.

* * * *

I barely managed to keep the contents of my stomach down. Under the tarp was a rotten carcass. It looked like it might have been a deer. Its flesh hung in tatters and maggots crawled over it, wriggling in the ecstasy of an endless food supply. I dropped the tarp and stepped back, moving away from the foul smell as quickly as I was able.

Once clear, I filled my lungs with clean fresh air, revelling in the contrast. Why would anyone dump a dead animal, and then cover it up? Did it die there? Or maybe it was to mask something else? Could that be it? The path continued into the nearby forest. I could see a single bare footprint in the mud. It was too small to be made by Fetun. On an impulse, I followed the path.

It went arrow straight for a hundred meters, heading into the heart of the forest, but then it turned slowly, until it ran more easterly. No matter; if it was just one path there was no chance of getting lost on it. I followed as it twisted and turned, all the while looking for any sign of freshly disturbed earth. You never knew. It would be quite the story if I actually found a body.

After about half an hour, I gave up and decided to go back to the farm. But when I turned, I was astonished to see that at the point where the path changed direction, there was a branch and the path split. I don't understand how I could have missed that, and for the life of me, I couldn't figure out which path to take.

I cursed my stupidity, and followed what I thought was the correct general direction. My stomach growled. Suddenly my next meal seemed a lot further away. The evening was still warm, even if the forest was getting rather gloomy. What sun there was, struggled to make it down as far as the forest floor, so I had to watch where I put my feet. Last thing I needed was a twisted ankle.

I took a left, at random and followed it for a few minutes. That was when I heard the first howl. The hair on my neck stood on end, and I had that peculiar experience of feeling my balls shrivel. Wolves were not common, but there were several packs in the northern forests. My thoughts went back to the deer. It was too decomposed to easily see what had killed it, but it did seem as if something had ripped out its guts. In spite of the warmth, I shivered. Another wolf howled, this time from a different direction. I panicked and started to run.

A third wolf howled, but this time it was ahead of me and I knew I was in trouble. They could smell prey from several kilometres. God knew how close they were, but I did not want to find out. I kept running, but with my physical conditioning it would not be long before I was exhausted.

There were more howls, coming from all around, and I desperately scanned the trees for a low branch. Maybe if I could climb up high enough, I would be safe. But every tree within sight sprouted branches so far above my head that climbing was an impossibility.

I ran on, fear giving me speed, if not endurance. Before very long I slowed, then stopped. Bending over, with hands on knees, I heaved, my breathing ragged. That's when I saw them.

* * * *

"Goddamn you, Fetun!" the officer dropped the cup he was holding. It fell the floor, smashing, tea splattering his trousers and shoes.

"Help! We've got a topper!"

Instantly booted feet came running. They all knew what that meant. *Topper*, prison slang for suicide. They had fucked up. He should have been on suicide watch. The first guard got the door to the cell open and rushed inside, lifting Fetun by his legs. Two more officers entered, and manhandled the prisoner to the ground. They immediately began CPR, one pounding the chest, another breathing air into the lungs. The third ran back out to call for an ambulance. It would not be needed. Fetun was not coming back.

"Shit," said the first guard. "We're in a fuck load of trouble now." He sat back and leaned against the bed. The other shook his head. Not in disagreement, but denial of the situation.

"Faen. Five minutes. He was alone for five fucking minutes."

"Where'd Sven go?"

"Call an ambulance, I would think."

"Jesus . . . I guess Fetun just couldn't live with himself."

"You know, that's the funny thing. I heard one of them Crown prosecutors saying that they didn't really have a case, and he was sure to walk."

* * * *

The wolf came slowly, moving between the trees with a casual grace, its eyes never leaving mine. It was beautiful; a grey black animal that looked exactly like the dog an ex-girlfriend had once had. But that mutt wouldn't rip your throat out and feast. This one planned to do exactly that.

I could hear movement around me. More grey shapes, flitting almost silently through the trees. I was surrounded. Too tired to be terrified, I knew I couldn't fight them, and that I was going to be an easy kill. I just hoped it would be quick. My mind and heart were racing, but my breath came in short, sharp pants, and I started to hyperventilate. The first wolf stepped closer, its lips curling back in a snarl. Then it stopped, raising its muzzle to sniff the air. I could hear whining from several of the creatures and I looked around to see that they too could smell something, and they didn't like it.

I looked back to the first wolf, and it was gone. It had turned and streaked away with unbelievable speed, the whole pack flowing around me, following their leader. I could not understand it at first, but something had clearly spooked them. Then I heard a voice, high and clear and pure. A girl singing in the forest. For a second I thought of red riding hood, and almost giggled. I was on the edge of hysteria.

The voice got louder and before long, I could see her through the trees. A young woman, dressed in a long dark skirt and white blouse. I wondered if she was coming back from a party, or wedding or something. I will be the first to admit that I am not an expert on the Bunad, the traditional national dress, but it was a type I had never seen before. The skirt was tied around her waist with an embroidered belt, from which hung a little silver purse. Her peasant style blouse was ornate with fine stitching. She was barefoot, but in her hand, she held a basket. She saw me and stopped singing, her mouth blossoming into a wide smile.

As she approached, she tilted her head first to one side, then the other, as if to get a better look at me from a different angle. With the wolves gone, I had started to regain my composure and I took a shuddering breath, waving my hands idiotically.

"It's not safe. There's wolves here. They might come back . . ."

She held up her hand and I fell silent. "They won't hurt you. Not if you're with me. I won't let them."

She put down the basket and I could see it was full of blueberries. Dark, almost black in the dimming light. She saw my gaze and smiled again.

"You look hungry. Sit with me. You can have something to eat and drink and you can rest a while."

I shook my head. "I need to get back. I have to get home. I have work to do and there's . . ."

She raised her eyes to meet mine. I was electrified. So dark, so lovely.

"Come," she said. "Just rest a while with me, and I will take you back to your conveyance."

"My car . . . you mean my car."

"Yes. I will take you back to your car. But first, sit with me here. There is time enough for work and time enough for love. Tell me your name."

I sank to the ground, grateful for the opportunity to rest. My legs were like rubber after the experience with the wolves. She sat next to me, eyes never leaving mine, her head tilting slightly, the smile widening to show even white teeth that all seemed to be ever so slightly pointed.

"Eirik," I said. "My name is Eirik"

"Such a strong name, such a strong man to run from wolves." She leaned towards me, her voice now a whisper, warm against my ear. "Rest my lovely. You will need your strength."

The young woman, her eyes impossibly big, her lips pressing onto mine.

* * * *

How I came to be in my car, I don't know. I drove carefully back down the mud road, until it became gravel and then tarmac again. I got back onto the highway and headed to Hamar. I would stay the night in a hotel, then go home the next day. Thinking back to the forest, and the wolves and the girl, it seemed like a dream. I could not even remember her face. She was beautiful, but why could I not remember her face?

My back muscles ached, as if I had been exercising hard. Of course, I had been running. That must be it. I kept seeing an image of a girl with dark eyes that looked into my soul. She had kissed me. Kissed me, then pushed me onto my back. I don't know why, but I felt incredibly satisfied.

* * * *

The ringing of my phone woke me from the most pleasant dream I had ever had. I don't remember what it was, but I was distraught at being forced to leave it. I staggered over to my phone and picked it up.

"Yeah?"

"Eirik. I've been trying you all night. Where you been?"

"Sleeping. What is it Bjorn?"

"Did you hear about Fetun?"

"Sure. He's crazy. I put it in the article."

"No! He killed himself. With his own belt."

I had not expected that, and I felt as if someone had kicked me in the gut. "Shit."

"Exactly. I need you to go back to Hamar and talk to the guards. Find out if he said anything to them before he pulled the plug."

"I'm still in Hamar."

"Good. Get with it."

I ended the call and closed my eyes. Isaak Fetun was not a killer, I was sure. But he had killed himself rather than risk giving away anything more than he already had. I played back the interview I had made with him. Hearing his voice, knowing he was dead was strange. I felt slightly guilty listening, as if I had done this thing to him and it was immoral to listen to the echoes of a dead man.

"She came from the forest, and she went back to the forest."

He died to protect his daughter. She would not be found, unless she wanted to be found. My thoughts, unbidden, went to the girl I had met. Did she want to be found? Why did the wolves fear her?

I was not going to find out, and I tried to put it out of my head. I took a shower, got dressed and went and interviewed the duty officers when Fetun was brought in. I sent what I had to Bjorn and drove home. I didn't give it any more thought. There was a bottle waiting, and I was eager to see it.

* * * *

As the months passed, I ascribed the whole experience to a kind of hysteria. Sure, it was sad about Isaak. He shouldn't have died. But he chose that path rather than to . . . I had to stop thinking about it. There was no point in trying to understand why a crazy man does anything. And he *was* crazy. He had to be.

I threw myself into my work and a bottle and forgot about the time I was terrorised by wolves, and seduced by a beautiful girl in a forest. I put it out of my head and in time came to think of it as just a dream. Until it came unbidden to my door in the middle of the night.

The knock was gentle but insistent. I was not sleeping, but I was bleary eyed when I cracked the door open. The sight that greeted me was mildly alarming.

She was old, clearly toothless, with a wild profusion of hair on her chin.

The old woman was wrapped in a cloak of tattered grey and black wool that covered her almost like a burqa, without the veil. She was very small, and she looked up at me with glittering eyes, smiling toothlessly.

"You'll be inviting me in, young man. I have words you'll be wanting to hear."

I shook my head in confusion. What could she have to do with me?

"Uh, I don't think so. What exactly . . ." Before I could finish, she pushed past me and shut the door behind her. I caught sight of a leathery brown arm and gnarled hand.

"Who are you? What do you want?" The reporter's instinct to ask questions was usually a good thing, but this time I wondered if I would regret my inquisitive nature. She pulled aside the heavy wool cloak, and I could see she was holding something in her other arm, cradling it like a football.

"She's yours, young man. Your flesh and your blood. By your balls and your cock, you made a fine little baby."

She held the small bundle out for me to see, and I stared in horrified fascination. How could I be a father? And who the hell was this old crone? I watched as her stick like fingers pulled away the blanket that shrouded the child and for the first time I saw her face. Dark eyes looking into mine. Big, beautiful eyes that could see into my soul. She was mine. In my gut, in my heart, in every part of my being, I knew that she was my daughter.

I held out my hands and the old woman placed the baby carefully into my arms. "You ware these words now, young man. She came from the forest, and she'll go back to the forest, when the time is right. Until then, you're her ward. You'll keep her safe, and you'll never tell another living soul her secret. Not if you don't want your cock to shrivel and drop off. There be curses for betrayers and that's the least of 'em."

"What? Oh yes, of course. I won't tell anybody. Can I hold her?"

The old woman snorted derisively. "Course you can. How you gonna bathe her otherwise?" She pulled the blanket part way open. I could see the baby's hands. So small and delicate. I counted ten fingers and ten tiny nails. Perfect.

"She's lovely. What's her name," I said, as I put my little finger into her fist. She clutched it tightly and regarded me with an adoring gaze and I felt myself smiling back at her.

"She is a child of the forest. We don't give 'em names. That's for you to decide."

"Brighitta," I said, pulling the blanket back, intent on counting her little toes too. And there, wrapping itself around one chubby leg, was a tiny tail. It curled around the child's thigh and twitched. I stared, not breathing. The baby released my finger and put its thumb into its mouth, beginning to suckle. She yawned, and the tail flexed casually, then stretched out, wrapping itself around my finger, holding me.

I don't know how long I stood there staring down at my strange little girl, but when I looked up the old woman was gone. She had done her job. She had delivered the baby. And I was its father.

It's time soon for Brighitta to go back to the forest. And when she does I don't know what I'll do. She has been my everything these last eighteen years, and I cannot imagine life without her. When she leaves, maybe I'll go back to Fetun's farm and take a walk in the woods. And if the wolves find me, well, that's fine. But maybe I'll meet Brighitta's mother again, picking blueberries and singing and that would be fine too. If anyone ever reads this journal, then it is a sure bet that either the wolves got me, or she did.

Fossegrim

You hear a loon's cry where river
swirls in lonely morning mist,
by rocks where she drowned last
summer, golden hair tangled in sticks
and river mud. And now wind spirits
away the silence of trees. Is this
her voice you hear, or a faint fiddle
tune blending with river's endless
rush? Where on this earth can you lay
your head, now that her empty cairn
echoes long through winter nights?
Let water sweep away your endless
tears. River's embrace, cold but tender,
teaches magic of memory and peace.
Let go. Even in grief's fearsome grip
you dance to this wild and mournful tune.

By Steve Klepetar

Haute Cuisine

Gregg Chamberlain

In the grey gloom of the hour before dawn, a three-headed troll slouched uphill towards its cave. Dark clouds in the overcast sky promised rain, which suited the troll's sour mood.

"Bloody waste of a night," grumbled the right-hand head. "Nothin' to show for all that work but one scrawny carcass."

The centre head nodded in agreement while the one on the far left snorted and rolled his eyes before turning a bit to check and make sure the troll's left hand had a firm grip on the half-naked man, tied up with strips of cloth and leather, draped still and silent over a shoulder. Tucked under the troll's right arm, chinking and clinking with every step, was a mass of broken Aesir mail.

Ducking down to enter the cave, the troll paused for a moment to glance around. Grunting in satisfaction at seeing no sign of intruders or unwelcome visitors, the troll let its burden slide down off its shoulder and drop to the floor. A shove of one big foot sent the still-unconscious man sliding further inside the cave, fetching up against one of the damp walls. A fling of the troll's right arm sent the mess of mail flying also, to land clashing and chiming on the cave floor close by.

"Hunh unnnh" grunted the right-hand head, as the troll twisted then shoved an arm behind its back and stretched until there came a loud crack. "Oh, that's better." It plopped down where it stood, then, after a moment, lifted up one foot, set that across a knee, and began massaging with both hands between the horny, callused toes.

"Ah, that's nice that is," murmured the centre head. The left-hand head nodded, eyes half-closed.

"Bloody feet ache all the time," muttered the right-hand head. The left-hand head scoffed.

"Complain, complain, complain," he growled. "All the time with you, Hagrumb, it's moan, moan, moan. You don't hear us grousing now, do yeh?"

"He wouldn't hear us anyway, Hegrumb," said the centre head.

"True enough, Hogrumb," agreed Hegrumb, smirking. "He'd never shut up long enough to listen."

The right-hand head glared at his siblings. "Maybe I should be shutting you lot up," Hagrumb threatened, looking down where the hands were now massaging the other foot. The fingers of the left hand stopped working away between two toes, clenched into a tight fist then froze just as the arm started to lift up.

Hagrumb grunted, eyes squinting, staring at the fist. But it refused to move any further. "Aw, nobbles to both of ya, fine then, I give up," Hagrumb grumbled, glancing over at his sibling heads. "Always ganging up on me, you two are, and don't give me that 'Who, me?' look, Hogrumb, 'cause you bloody well knows what I mean."

Turning away from his siblings—the one smiling sheepishly, the other sneering and snorting—Hagrumb watched as both hands resumed their massage work. "Well, then," he said at last. "What we gonna do for dinner tonight?"

Hegrumb's ragged mouth pursed in thought. Hogrumb jerked his head over at a small piece of wood shoved into the dirt of a cave wall that served as a shelf for a single solitary book. "Let's try a new recipe," he said.

The other two heads each turned towards their middle sibling. "It's just us here," growled Hegrumb. "Why go to all that trouble?"

"Yeah," agreed Hagrumb. "Be different if we had us some company. Not that anyone ever comes to visit."

"And who's to blame for that?" retorted Hogrumb. "You bit the head off the last person came to see us before she even had a chance to say 'hello'."

"That were just one o' those wretched old hags an' it weren't my fault," answered Hagrumb. "She startled me, sneaking up from behind like that. Yer knows I don't like being surprised."

"Got a point, Hagrumb does," conceded Hegrumb. "She did come up on us sly-like. No 'view, halloo' ner nothin'."

"Well, I'm in the mood for something different tonight," argued Hogrumb. "It has been a right muck of a night, I agree, and something a bit special is just the thing we all need, I'm thinking."

The other two heads muttered a bit but made no further objections. The troll got to its feet, went over to the shelf and picked up the well-worn copy of *Childe's Guide to Fine Dining* sitting there. It stood, leafing through the pages, each head studying the pictures for the recipes as they flicked past.

"We could try this, 'Oliver's Buttermilk Roast Chicken'," suggested Hagrumb.

Hogrumb shook his head. "Now that's no good. You know very well I'm lactose intolerant!"

More pages flipped.

"Here's a possible," exclaimed Hegrumb. "Boeuf Bourguignon Bordeaux."

Hagrumb squinted at the page and grimaced. "Red wine gives me awful migraines."

"We could always do a nice Tuscan ragoût.," Hogrumb mumbled. The other two heads turned and glared at him.

"After six nights of mutton stew?" Hegrumb scowled. "I don't think so."

All three heads sighed.

"Well, I guess that settles it," Hagrumb grumbled.

"And after all that hard work, what with the tenderizing and the peeling," groused Hegrumb, examining one set of skinned knuckles.

All three heads looked over at the battered and bruised Aesir, now awake and aware, huddled against the dank cave wall. Bound and gagged, shivering and quivering, beside the broken remains of his armour, he tried in vain to make himself seem smaller and less noticeable.

"Right then, fellows," declared Hogrumb. "Looks like it's sushi tonight!"

Troll Boat

Winging through water,
the Troll boat sails
down from mountains
to green fields,
where lonely farmsteads
lie not far from the sea.
Down the river
they plunge with fiery eyes,
and mouths redder
than cabbage leaves.
They drum as they come.
Troll father, with his green
beard, roars.
His wife, with her fishhook
Nose, has baked hard bread
to serve with salted fish.
His son's hands have hardened
into stone, while his daughter sings
her lust, drinking the fiery water of life.

By Steve Klepetar

Draugr's Saga

Hugh B. Long

Under an iron sky, frigid waves besieged the longship, leaping over the sides of the boat and assaulting the warriors inside. The gods had smiled on them for the first three days of their voyage, providing clear skies and generous winds. On the fourth day Aegir's fury was a terror to experience, for Aegir was a god of the sea, and the water was his kingdom. Men crossed his realm at their peril.

The crew had long since reefed the sail and now focused on steering her into the waves that rose like mountains and fell like valleys. Foolish sailors might have steered for shore, but in strange waters, no man knew where deadly rocks or other hazards might lurk just beneath the surface, waiting to bring them to Aegir's kingdom beneath the waves.

For hours, Arndt Bjarnisson did battle with the massive steering-oar. It kicked and jarred him. On several occasions, it bucked and swung so violently that only the ropes lashing Arndt to the oar kept him from being thrown overboard. Many offered up to Aegir's nine daughters what little they had in their stomachs. Great streaks of light flashed across the sky. They could hear Thor doing battle with the frost giants in the heavens above, his hammer thundering with each blow.

For three torturous days and two frozen nights, the crew hung to slim hope, yet finally, the storm abated. They were spent, their woolen tunics heavy with seawater, their bellies empty and their spirits black.

Although the rain relented, a dark blanket of cloud yet hung over them menacingly, blocking their view of the sun, making navigation difficult.

Erik Sigurdsson was a big man, even by the standards of his hardy people. He wore his straw colored hair and beard long, both braided with silver beads. His handsome face was still clear of scars, though he had fought in a shield-wall. This was his first summer raid commanding his own ship. He had previously accompanied his father on raids for five summers and acquitted himself bravely, thusly earning the silver to purchase his own boat. It wasn't newly built, but the *Ottar* was Erik's. These were his karls, his warriors, and he their Jarl's son. Out of respect, they addressed him as Lord, but until his father died, he was their equal in the law of the Northmen, despite his father's status.

Erik stood on the raised steering platform at the stern of the longship, gazing out over the vast sea.

"What do you see, Lord?" asked Sven Gardarsson, a grizzled veteran.

"Little of nothing, Sven. Aegir has seen fit to blow us well off course." Erik pulled a yellowish crystal from a pouch on his belt and held it up to his eye. As he held the sunstone up, he turned his body in a circle until it glowed, indicating the direction of the sun; now they at least knew their direction of travel. "Keep us on a westerly course, Sven. I believe we should still be close to Ireland. My cousin Thorfinn is awaiting our arrival. I do not want to disappoint him."

"Aye, Lord." Sven put his shoulder into the steering-oar and the *Ottar's* clinker-built hull groaned as she flexed and rippled under pressure from the pounding waves, slowly turning onto a westerly course.

Erik could hear his men laughing, which was usually a good sign. After three days battling the storm, they were thirsty, hungry and tired. A fire was flickering in a brazier mounted above one of the benches. Good, he thought. Some hot soup would be nice.

* * * *

Ivar Haraldsson laughed at Aedan. "You sad little bastard! Look! He pissed himself," Ivar said, pointing to Aedan's stained crotch. Aedan had been a thrall, a slave, but was now a freed man. Erik's father, Sigurd, had captured Aedan during a raid on Ireland seven years past, and had freed him just this spring. He was like a little brother to Erik, but as a former thrall was not well regarded by the karls—Aedan had yet to prove himself in battle.

Ivar was laughing and encouraging the other men to join his mockery. Aedan watched with shame as Erik strode down to the middle deck near the fire and stood beside Ivar, who was a hand taller and significantly bigger built than Erik.

"What reverie have I missed?" Erik asked, with a curious smile.

"We were just noticing evidence of the thrall's courage," Ivar said grinning. "See, he pissed himself." He pointed to Aedan's trousers, looking around for support.

"I see," Erik nodded. "Is that a trick you taught him, Ivar? I seem to remember you pissing yourself a couple of summers ago in the shield wall." Erik spoke evenly, raising an eyebrow. "And if I am not mistaken, he is a thrall no longer. Your Jarl freed him just this spring. Are you so old that this memory escapes you?" Aedan had been freed owing to his diligent work on Sigurd's farmstead. In the North, actions spoke louder than accidents of birth.

Ivar's face flushed red with fury, his hand going to the handle of his seax where it hung from his belt.

"I had to piss before that battle," he seethed. "I drank much ale with the men to celebrate our upcoming victory."

Erik nodded slyly. "I hear ale does help build courage. Did it work?"

Ivar drew his seax in a flash, but just as fast, a man behind him grabbed his sword arm and a second grabbed his shield arm, dragging him back. Ivar frothed at the mouth.

Erik maintained an outward calm, appearing to any onlookers to be completely unfazed by this attempted assault. "Excellent, Ivar! Let us hope you can muster that same fury in the face of the Irish." Erik stepped forward, standing nose to nose with Ivar as the others held him. "Draw a blade on me again, you puddle of weasel piss, and I'll cut off your balls and feed them to you." He patted Ivar on the shoulder and smiled.

Ivar's face relaxed. Had Ivar's blade reached Erik, he would have been lucky to survive the encounter, unless he struck a lucky blow—Erik was a formidable warrior—had he miraculously killed Erik, his karls would have been honor bound to kill Ivar. Either way, Ivar would have died.

Ivar shook off his saviors and skulked off to the prow of the ship.

Aedan offered Erik a cup of soup. "Thank you, Aedan," Erik said.

As the youngest crewman, Aedan was relegated to performing some of the more menial tasks during the voyage. Since he had seven years experience with such drudgery, he took on those tasks willingly. Aedan had done everything asked of him, in order to earn some silver on this voyage. He had been conflicted when he was first chosen to go on this raid, as they would plunder his own countrymen. Because Aedan was so young when he was taken from his home, he eventually accepted his feelings that he was more at home in the fjords and mountains, than in the hills of Ireland.

Erik sipped the steaming soup gingerly. "How is it?" Aedan asked.

"Tastes like hot piss. But it's warm." He winked at Aedan.

Aedan loved his foster brother. He was a few years younger than Erik, but the boys had spent seven years together growing up on the same farmstead. Erik's father always treated Aedan well. All the thralls on Sigurd's farmstead were treated with dignity. He brooked no disrespect or disobedience, but if they worked hard, they were treated like family and eventually freed.

"Erik!" A young man named Einar yelled out. "Land!"

Erik and Aedan made their way back to the steering platform, which was raised above the rowing benches. Aedan could indeed see land. He just hoped it was Ireland.

* * * *

As the *Ottar* slid onto the unknown shore, several of the men leaped into the surf, dragging her onto the strand and beaching her. Erik, now wearing mail armor, sword, and shield, jumped from the prow onto the rocky beach. Aedan followed.

Erik was surveying the terrain inland as Sven strode up and stood beside them.

"My Lord, is this Ireland?"

"Look around, Sven. Tell me what you see," Erik said.

Sven appeared tentative, but attempted an answer. "Grass and sand, my Lord?"

"There are no trees. Not a single tree." Erik looked to Sven. "What do you make of that?"

"Perhaps the Celts cut them down?" Sven offered.

"All of them?" Aedan asked. "Then where are the stumps?"

Erik nodded at his foster brother. "Just so."

Aedan walked with Erik and Sven as they patrolled the beach for an hour in each direction. They saw not a single tree or shrub. There were grassy mounds everywhere, as far as they could see inland. It was like a rolling sea of green waves. Erik told Aedan it was the strangest land he'd ever seen. Each mound was tall enough so that they could not see from valley to valley.

Back at the *Ottar*, Erik ordered the men to make camp for the night. They pitched tents and started a proper fire that warmed them all. Thankfully, there was a great supply of driftwood.

Erik, and steersman Arndt, pitched their tent. More tents bloomed, arranged in a semi-circle around the fire. Aedan shared a tent with a young man named Gjurd Sigurdsson, who was no direct relation to Erik.

Tonight would mark the first hot meal in several days—not counting the soup Aedan had made. To improve spirits, Erik broke out a small barrel of his own mead to share with the men. Around the fire, men told tales of shield wall bravado, maidens conquered and treasure found. Erik mentioned that some of the tales from previous summers seemed to grow more impossible with each telling.

"What do you intend for tomorrow, Erik?" Aedan asked.

"Njord and Aegir permitting, we shall sail north up the coast until we see something familiar."

Aedan sipped his mead and enjoyed the mélange of scents the beach provided; the salt air, seaweed, the smell of word burning. These were comforting and familiar.

"Hear me," Erik said in a low voice, "the next time that bastard insults you, challenge him. Do not allow your honor to be shit upon. You are part of Sigurd's household. Even though you are not his son by blood, your acts are tied to our family. Do you understand?"

Aedan nodded, feeling shame for his lack of action.

"I love you as if you were my brother by blood. I will back you in any fight. You are a freed man—act like it."

Seven years of being subservient had left Aedan meek. Aedan was not used to having the option of speaking back when insulted, and although Erik had trained with him recently, he was very new to handling a sword. By contrast, Erik had been taught to hold a blade from the time he could walk.

"I shall try, Erik. I promise."

* * * *

Longships are symmetrical, such that they can be rowed or sailed equally well in either direction. In the morning when they departed, they didn't need to turn the Ottar around. They had but to man the oars, give her a push, and they'd be away.

Aedan labored to set up camp with the men, erecting an A-frame to hang the linen tent. It was imbued with sheep fat and stank, but they shed water well and kept the winds at bay. With the camp setup complete, Aedan mingled with the men, seeing to any final needs. He spied old man Svolnir. He was the oldest man Aedan had ever seen, with hair as white as spider's silk, and a face like worn saddle leather and a frail body. Almost every man on this crew was a warrior, except for Valmar, an apprentice shipbuilder, brought along to repair the Ottar as needed. But where Valmar was fit enough to row, Svolnir was not.

"Good evening, Svolnir," Aedan said as he passed the man's fire.

Svolnir nodded and smiled, threatening to crack his weathered face.

Aedan noted he was fiddling with a leather pouch and saw tiles of wood spill out into the old man's hand—runes. "Can you read them?"

Svolnir grinned widely now, showing off his one remaining tooth. "Of course, boy," he croaked.

Aedan sat cross-legged beside him. "Can you read my future?"

"The young are ever curious," he said. "When you get to my age you don't want to know what tomorrow brings, for it's always more aches and pains, and death around the corner. Better to enjoy each breath as you can."

Aedan was seventeen winters and not overly worried about aches and pains just yet. It occurred to him that the Northmen counted age in winters, and the Irish in summers. Odd.

"Can you teach me how to read them?" Aedan asked.

"Certainly. I am a skilled Urdskapar—Wyrd Shaper."

Aedan beamed. Wyrd was the Northmen's name for fate, or destiny, though it was different in that you could shape it. Which was why men sought to know what their wyrd held, then with a good reading they could take action to change their future.

"And in ten years you might be able to cast them properly," Svolnir continued.

Aedan's hopes fell. "Well, can you just read my future then? Tell me, will I earn silver on this voyage? Or fame?"

"A gift for a gift, boy," Svolnir said.

Aedan had heard that maxim before. The Norse gods demanded a gift for a gift. If you wanted their help, then you made appropriate sacrifices to them to ensure your pleas were heard. Aedan had nothing of value to give the old man. His clothes were rags, and he owned no weapons, save for a rusty belt knife. "I own nothing of value," he said, disappointed.

The old man shrugged.

But then Aedan remembered something. He reached into his almost empty belt pouch and retrieved a small chunk of hack silver, the size of his thumbnail. It had been a small piece of an arm ring that had been hacked off to pay for something. Arm rings were the Northmen's preferred method of carrying wealth. They were portable, and could be divided as required. But that was all he had. It had been a gift from Erik's father, Sigurd, to give him luck on his journey.

He proffered it to the old man with regret and shame, for it was not much of a gift. But to his surprise, Svolnir smiled and nodded, taking the chunk of metal.

"A gift for a gift," Svolnir intoned. He lay sheet of tan linen on the ground in front of him, then looked up at Aedan. "You must ask me a question before I cast the runes. The more specific the question, the better the reading will be. Understand?"

Aedan nodded.

"Then tell the Norns what you would know."

Aedan had to consider that. What did he want to know? If he asked whether or not he'd get any silver, maybe he would get a yes, but how much? Maybe he'd get two coins. He'd heard that these readings could be tricky. What did he really want to know?

"How can I become wealthy this summer?" If the Norns answered that, then all his problems would be solved. All he dreamed of now was enough silver to start a new life. He'd stay in the North, likely. Or maybe settle in one of the Norse controlled areas of Ireland. He felt more Norse than Irish now, and had never considered returning to the monastery. What was there for him? They were his keepers, not his family. He didn't even know who his family were. And most of those monks had probably been killed or enslaved when he had been captured. No, Sigurd and Erik were his only real family now. But wives and land cost silver. He'd never inherit anything from Sigurd, so he had to secure his own fortune.

Svolnir nodded. "Since you are a Christian-"

"I am not Christian!" Aedan interrupted, and pulled his Thor's hammer amulet from beneath his tunic. "Do you see a crucifix around my neck, or Mjolnir?" he demanded.

Svolnir lifted his hands up placatingly. "Be calm, boy, I meant no offense. But since you are from Ireland, and were a Christian, I shall do the reading according to your Urd, your past, where you came from. That is important."

Aedan nodded.

"Do you know how these rune tiles are made, boy?"

"They're carved from the wood of a fruit tree?"

"More than that. An Urdskapar must craft his own set of runes. Under a full moon he must harvest the wood for the tiles, making an offering to the tree and the earth for their gifts. Then, that same night he must carve them and stain them with his own blood as a sacrifice to the Norns and dedicate them to the gods. Only such tiles will ever prove useful. If a man tries to sell you runes, spit on him, for he is a thief and a liar."

Aedan nodded. He had no idea there was so much involved.

"I will draw six rune tiles and place them in the form of a celtic cross. I will tell you what each may mean, but only you will understand the full import of the rune. I have no knowledge of your life and troubles. Do you understand?"

Aedan nodded.

And so he began. Svolnir chanted as he thrust his hand into the leather bag holding the runes. "This first will represent the root of your problem." He drew the first tile and set it down. "Fehu it is called. It means wealth, such as cattle, gold. It can indicate prosperity."

That made perfect sense to Aedan. The root of his current problem was wealth, or its lack.

Svolnir pulled a second rune and placed it above the first. "Algiz it is called. A symbol of protection. This is where you should direct your energy to reach your goal."

Of course, Aedan might be in a shield-wall soon enough. He'd need to be careful and seek protection there.

A third he pulled and set above the second in a straight line. "The problems you face now are affected by Pertho, which signifies, birth, or chance."

He was an orphan, an ex-slave, and now a penniless freedman. Yes, that seemed to fit. His current situation was governed by accidents of birth and chance.

The fourth rune was placed above and to the right of the third, forming the first arm of the celtic cross. "This will help you over come your problems. Kenaz, it is called. It symbolizes fire and sometimes knowledge."

The fifth rune tile he placed across from the fourth, forming the second arm of the cross. "What are you still lacking? Mannaz. Men."

He pulled a final rune which he placed above them all, finishing the cross. "Hagalaz represents the outcome of your summer." Svolnir looked concerned and lowered his head.

"What is it? What does Hagalaz mean?"

The old man looked up, appearing suddenly weary. "Hail, destruction. Drastic change."

"Then perhaps I will destroy my enemies? That's good, isn't it?"

"Perhaps," Svolnir said grudgingly. "Though, I've rarely seen men succeed after Hagalaz appears. It's also a rune for the queen of the dead, Hella, ruler of Hellheim."

* * * *

Every night when the men were away from their homes and raiding, they posted a watch. There was always a chance that they would be attacked by locals. Their gravest worry was that some sneaky Celt would set fire to their boat. If the *Ottar* were destroyed they would be stranded in a foreign land, unable to flee their foes; the longship's greatest strength was its ability to strike anywhere, then flee quickly.

During the first watch, an hour after the first men lay down to get some sleep, screaming caused the guards to sound their horns.

Aedan threw off his blanket and scrambled out of the tent. He saw Erik standing outside as well, sword in hand.

"What is happening?" Erik demanded of a sentry.

"I am not sure, Lord. We heard screaming from over near that mound," a sentry said, pointing.

Several other men scrambled out of their tents. Erik pointed to one of them. "You! Get four more men to come with me." The designated man scrambled back into his tent to grab his sword, then dashed off to gather some men.

Aedan accompanied Erik and four of his men as they walked cautiously toward the source of the commotion. Each had their weapon ready, whether a sword, a spear or axe. They scrambled up and down two mounds until they saw a torch laying on the ground and a man beside it—Ivar.

"What in Niflheim are you doing?" Erik snapped. Ivar sat panting, gasping for breath and holding his wrist.

"It atta - attacked us," he stammered

"Who attacked you?" Erik demanded. The other men were looking around, now on high alert. It was not unheard of for villagers to kill a straggler from camp. Some got brave while the bulk of the Northmen were sleeping.

"It came out of the mound. I tried to fight it off, but it got Gjurd!" Ivar trembled visibly as he spoke.

"Where is Gjurd?" Erik asked

"At the mound"

"We're surrounded by bloody mounds, you fool! Which mound? Where? Point or something," Erik said exasperated, then turned to Aedan. "Help him up."

Aedan reluctantly helped Ivar to his feet. When he saw it was Aedan, Ivar pushed him away.

Erik glared at Ivar. "Lead us to him."

Ivar, still trembling, and glancing back to ensure he wasn't alone, walked hesitantly up the hill and west.

Six mounds over they found Gjurd in front of a hole. He was bloodied and lying still. As they got closer they saw a large wound on his neck. A freshly dug pile of dirt lay beside the hole.

"Did you two badgers dig this hole?" Erik asked, contempt dragging the words from his mouth.

Ivar opened and closed his mouth twice before finally speaking. "We- were exploring, and we saw a silver ring on the ground. We reckoned these might be burial mounds, so we dug a little, then found a few silver coins. We kept on digging and found a door to the mound. We knew there would be more gold and silver in there- for you, my Lord, of course." Ivar grimaced. "But ... we found something else. There was a corpse in the mound."

"What in Niflheim did you expect to find in a grave mound?" Erik shook his head.

One of his karls examined Gjurd as they spoke.

"Is he dead?" Erik asked

"Aye, Lord. Good and dead. There is a chunk bit clean out of his neck. Looks like teeth marks—a man's teeth."

Erik glared at Ivar and Aedan had a sinking feeling. Was this man a cannibal? He had heard stories.

Gjurd twitched, and the man examining him jumped back, startled.

"Good and dead you say?" Erik asked and spat. "Has my whole crew lost sense tonight? Take Gjurd back to camp and tend to his wound. And take Ivar back as well, looks like he injured his wrist." Erik stormed back off to camp.

* * * *

Aedan trudged slowly behind the men as they returned to camp, allowing them to pull ahead. Once there was enough distance between them and the light from their torches no longer overlapped, he turned and dashed back to the grave. Curiosity overwhelmed Aedan's good sense. If it *was* a grave mound, there might very well be treasure in there. Great lords were buried with their best weapons, gold, and even slaves and animals. Surely a peek wouldn't hurt, he thought.

He crept up to the freshly dug hole, his torch thrust well ahead to light the way. He struggled through the small hole and peered deeper into the mound. He had hoped he would be able to see enough from the entrance to judge whether crawling further was in order, but a bend in the tunnel prevented a straight view in.

Aedan continued crawling on all fours for a time. Once he made his way to the bend, he peered around the corner. What he saw sent a chill through his whole body, freezing him like a stiff winter wind. There was a corpse ahead of him, though why that bothered him, he did not know. It was a grave mound and he'd seen corpses before.

Clothed in fetid purple-robes, a long-seax had been thrust up through its chin, the tip protruding from the top of its skull. The corpse was shriveled and desiccated. The other two probably just panicked. But how did Gjurd get the bite on his neck? Surely Ivar didn't do that?

He took note of the corpse's tattered raiment. They looked as if they might have been worn by someone of very high station. Purple was often worn by the wealthy—a king perhaps? Sadly there was no king's treasure that he could see.

He steeled himself, touching the Thor's hammer amulet—Mjolnir— around his neck. Thor was a northern god, said to be a friend and protector of mankind, and Aedan craved his protection just then. He crawled past the corpse, averting his gaze and made his way into the burial chamber. He was disappointed to find it empty. There were no mounds of silver and gold, no chests of jewels. The few coins Ivar found must have been the whole treasure. Thieves had likely robbed this mound ages ago.

All that remained were piles of moldy cloth wrappings that stank so much he had to suppress retching. Time to go, he reckoned.

As he made his way back out of the mound, Aedan came upon the corpse again, the long-seax still protruding from its skull. Although disgusted, he thought he ought to inspect the weapon. After all, it was more or less a sword, which he needed. His only blade was a crude knife. The long-seax was filthy, encrusted with countless years of dirt. After carefully extracting it from the corpse's skull, he wiped it off with the bottom of his tattered brown tunic. After a brief cleaning, his spirits began to soar as he saw the true nature of the old blade. It was no common weapon. Wavy patterns on the blade seemed to dance under the torch light. Upon further examination, he noticed intricate carvings on the ivory handle. The blade also had several runes on it, but he could not read them. Although he had mastered Greek and Latin, owing to his early years as a ward of a monastery. He resolved to ask Erik, he would know. What a treasure!

The long-seax was forged with a single edged blade, like the shorter seax, but was nearly the length of a proper sword. Many men actually preferred the long-seax in the shield wall, which was better suited for stabbing, in the fashion of the Romans. He remembered reading the exploits of the Legions. They were mighty warriors, and seemed a race of giants.

While he marveled at his luck, the corpse twitched. The movement startled Aedan, and he yelped like a girl. Without a second's hesitation, he scrambled out of the mound like a hare with its tail on fire.

* * * *

Back at camp, Aedan spied Erik sitting by a fire. He looked to be in a foul mood. Beside the fire, a young man was tending to Gjurd's wound, while the patient moaned and fidgeted.

"Gods, he reeks!" Aedan said.

"You all smell like goat shit after four days at sea," Erik said.

"No, Erik, he smells like death." Aedan nearly choked and stepped away from Gjurd, back towards Erik.

Gjurd continued moaning and seemed to be getting agitated.

"Erik," Aedan said in a whisper, "I found something." Aedan unwrapped the long-seax from the hem of his woolen tunic and showed Erik, while glancing around to make sure no others saw it.

"It has runes on it, but I cannot read them," Aedan said.

Erik motioned to Aedan and turned his back away from the fire and the other men. "Show me," he whispered.

Aedan slowly proffered his prize to Erik for inspection, hilt first.

Erik held the weapon at arm's length, allowing the firelight to flicker and dance on its blade. "This is a beautiful blade, Aedan."

"But what does it say?" Aedan asked impatiently.

"Just hold your tongue, you little goat turd, I shall get to it."

ᚦᚱᚠᚢᚷᚱᛋ • ᛒᚠᚾᛖ

Erik read each rune in turn, starting from the hilt and working towards the tip of the blade. "D, R, A, U, G, R, S, B, A, N, E." Erik had a look of shock on his face. "Aedan, this may be a very special weapon. It could have been made by the Svartalfar, the dark elves, in their underworld forges. The inscription reads 'Draugr's Bane'. You remember father's stories about the draugr?"

Aedan nodded. He remembered very well. Sigurd used to regale the children with stories of evil spirits who rose up from the dead to torment men—the draugar. Aedan thought they were only stories.

"This, my brother, is a weapon fit for a Jarl," Erik said.

Aedan felt a moment of panic shoot through his veins like ice water. Did Erik intend to keep it for himself?

"I hope you fight well with it, little brother," Erik said with a smile, handing the weapon back to Aedan.

Aedan beamed. As he admired his prize, he noticed more small marks near the modest cross guard. "Erik, there are other tiny marks," he held the hilt toward Erik and pointed, "here."

ᛁᛒᚠ

"Ah, a smith's mark. Likely the initials of the man who forged the blade. The runes are Isa, Berkana, and Ass. They mean ice, the birch tree, and the gods. They represent the letters I, B, and A. Maybe the smith was called Ivar something or other? Who knows."

Behind them Gjurd began to wail loudly and thrash like a beast. Erik and Aedan turned back to him.

"Poor bastard," Erik said. "He's probably been poisoned by Ivar's bite. I've seen men die from a bite suffered in battle. I knew of a man who's ear was bitten off by a Celt. He died a week later," Erik said.

As Aedan watched, he felt his hands grow warm. He looked down; there was a reddish glow surrounding the blade of his long-seax. "What in Muspellheim?" he said, invoking the name for the world of the fire giants.

The young man tending Gjurd screamed as Gjurd bit him. He jumped up and away from Gjurd. "You bastard! I was trying to help you!" he shouted.

Gjurd got to his feet and shambled after the young man. His eyes, Aedan noticed, were milky white orbs.

Erik ran up to Gjurd and grabbed him by the shoulder, spinning him around. As he did so, Gjurd bit Erik's wrist. Erik responded to the bite with a punch that would have leveled an ox. Gjurd fell, but immediately scrambled back up. Several other men wrestled Gjurd to the ground. They were soon yelling that they had been bitten.

"It seems Gjurd too, has a taste for men's flesh." Sven said. "My Lord, he's gone mad. It would be a kindness if we put him down."

"Aye," Erik said. He thought for a moment then unsheathed his sword. "Hold him down, and someone put a sword in his hand!" he ordered. A man who died without a weapon in hand might not go to Valhalla.

Four men held Gjurd's limbs, one pressing a sword into his immobilized hand, and Erik thrust his sword deep into the Gjurd's belly, clear through into the sand beneath him. But Gjurd continued to writhe and moan.

"Loki's spawn!" Erik cursed.

Erik thrust thrice more, and still, Gjurd continued to groan and thrash.

The men holding Gjurd leaped up and scrambled back, terrified at the *evil* in front of them. Gjurd ambled towards the group of men and several with spears held him at bay. Their spears pierced Gjurd's torso, but he kept pushing against them.

"He's a troll!" Sven shouted.

"Burn him!" One of the men shouted.

"You! Grab a torch!" Erik shouted.

One of his men tossed Erik a torch. He thrust it into Gjurd's back while Gjurd focused on another man who held him at bay with a spear. Gjurd's clothing burst into flame, but he appeared not to notice it at all.

One of the larger veterans, wielding a two-handed Danish axe, strode up to Gjurd and swung, cleaving him from shoulder to waist. Gjurd still refused to die! He was a smoking, shambling, half-split man, with one arm and shoulder drooping to the ground.

Several other men ran up, taking turns attacking Gjurd with seax, sword, spear and axe. None stopped him, but several were bitten and scratched in the process.

Aedan felt fear grip him, such as when he was small child. He let the other more experienced men make the initial attacks, but as they seemed to be wholly ineffective, he decided to act. He forced courage to the front of his mind and ran at Gjurd screaming a high pitched battle cry. He slashed at Gjurd with his long-seax, the blade glowing a bright red now. Gjurd screamed and howled for the first time—in pain! Aedan had hurt him, and Gjurd was on the retreat, but still he stood.

To Aedan's mind, Gjurd resembled a hacked and sliced pork roast—bits of his meat fell onto the strand as he moved around.

Aedan grabbed his long-seax with both hands and aimed a powerful blow at Gjurd's head and swung—The head came off as easily as knocking a jug off a wall. The blade's red glow flickered out and Gjurd ceased his thrashing.

* * * *

Exhausted, Aedan dropped to the ground and let his weapon sink onto the sand.

"Well done, brother!" Erik said, helping him up. He clapped Aedan on the shoulders.

Aedan retrieved his long-seax.

Erik beamed. "Come, you have well and truly earned some mead!" Erik explained Aedan's long-seax to the men, and its inscription. From this, they concluded that this had been no troll at all, but a draugr. The men cheered and gave thanks to Aedan, Draugr Slayer.

It was the middle of the night, but none of the men were going to get any rest, they were far too excited from their brush with the evil draugr. Several of the men burned the remains of Gjurd's body, just to be sure.

Fully half of Erik's crew had been wounded fighting Gjurd. Ivar had bandaged up his wrist, but was looking pale, and lay curled up in front of the fire.

"I never imagined Sigurd's tales were true, Erik." Aedan said.

"Nor I. We shall never doubt him again, eh?"

Aedan nodded.

"You were brave tonight," Erik said, "I was proud to call you my brother, and would be proud to call you my karl someday. In fact, I think we have some business to attend to."

Aedan looked puzzled as Erik stood.

"Men! Hear me! Tonight, I have a new brother. I, Erik Sigurdsson, take Aedan, freed man and Draugr Slayer, as my blood brother!" He motioned for Aedan to get up.

Aedan stood, mouth agape. Erik took Draugr's Bane from Aedan's hand and drew its blade sharply across his palm. Blood flowed freely from the long incision. He handed it back to Aedan, who assumed he was to do the same. He repeated the cut to his hand.

Erik then clasped his bloody palm to Aedan's, sealing the pact.

"Henceforth you shall be known as my blood-brother, Aedan Draugr Slayer. If any man disputes this, let him stand before me now." Erik glared into the crowd. The men seemed genuinely pleased for Aedan's elevation, and none came forward to challenge the adoption. Aedan had slain a draugr tonight—no man here could make that claim. And even though he was a young warrior with no experience in the shield wall, he had thrown himself into danger when needed. That was all the warriors needed to know. In the shield-wall, the man beside you could save your life or spell your doom. Aedan proved he could do the former.

Erik hugged him tightly, then grabbed at his stomach in sudden pain.

"Erik, are you well?" Aedan asked.

"Yes, yes, I shall be fine. Must have been that piss you fed me on the boat." Erik smiled weakly. "I just need to take some rest."

Several of the men seemed to be suffering from stomach ailments, and were variously groaning, writhing or clasping at their guts.

Erik went to his tent to lay down.

What had previously been a celebration now felt like the morning after.

Aedan sat quietly beside the fire, polishing Draugr's Bane, cleaning off the blood and gore. He caught Ivar on the other side of the fire, glaring back at him. He could feel the man's venomous stare as if they were a serpent's teeth sinking into his skin. Ivar was trouble, and Aedan knew their dealings were not yet concluded.

* * * *

Aedan crouched in front of the fire, at the edge of sleep, head nodding down. A shuffling sound alerted him. He watched Ivar stand then glanced down in his lap—Draugr's Bane glowed red. Aedan leaped to his feet.

Ivar's eyes were now dead milk-white orbs. They bored into his brain, and Ivar was . . . smiling!

"Erik!" Aedan shouted, while holding Draugr's Bane between him and his foe. Ivar shrank back when he saw the blade. "Hear me, you stinking piece of shit. I am Aedan, Draugr Slayer!" He paused as he saw Ivar's head twist and his shoulders flex. Was he getting bigger? Gods! Ivar was growing taller! And wider!

Erik stumbled out of his tent looking deathly pale. Several other men were up now, all looking seasick or hungover.

Ivar laughed at Aedan. He now stood at least a head above Erik, and was much wider.

"Men," shouted Erik weakly, "get to the boat. This place is cursed. I will hold Ivar. Go! You too, Aedan."

"No, I will not leave my brother!" Aedan said.

Erik thrust his sword deep into Ivar's back while he was focused on Aedan. Ivar reacted as if a fly had landed on him and back handed Erik, sending him flying into his tent, collapsing it.

Ivar pointed a rotting finger at Aedan. His flesh had begun to decay and the stench—it was worse than poor Gjurd.

Aedan slashed his long-seax at Ivar and lunged forward. A strong downward blow cut through Ivar's left wrist, severing it completely. Ivar howled, but did not retreat. Why was nobody helping him, Aedan wondered? There were over twenty men in camp and not one came to his aid. Useless bastards.

Aedan heard a noise behind him and saw one of the other crewmen, but he was not coming to help—his eyes were also milky white, and he stank. He was coming for Aedan as well.

"Erik! Help me!" Aedan screamed.

Erik picked himself up from the wreckage of his tent, and stumbled over to Aedan.

Aedan tried to keep both draugar in front him now. He knew he had to act decisively. He couldn't hope to fight two of them. He needed to kill one of them quickly. He saw an opening and lunged forward, swinging his long-seax, decapitating the other draugr. The headless corpse dropped to the ground like a sack of flour and moved no more.

That left Ivar. Aedan watched as Erik grabbed Ivar from behind in a bear hug, but Erik's arms would barely surround the creature now.

Ivar threw his head backward and Aedan heard a sickening wet crunch. Erik fell back to the sand, his face a bloody mess.

"Aedan, get to the ship," Erik croaked. He grabbed onto Ivar's ankles and held tight. "Go! Go!"

Aedan ran to the ship and saw men trying to push her into the waves—they were struggling. Aedan joined in, and his extra weight helped the *Ottar* slide off the strand and into the sea. He clambered aboard and fell onto the waterlogged deck.

He climbed to a sitting position and watched Erik stab his seax through Ivar's foot, pinning him to the ground.

As Ivar was held motionless, another shambling mass approached Erik from the direction of the mounds. Aedan blinked in recognition. It was the corpse from inside the mound.

"Erik! Leave him, run to the boat!" Aedan shouted, but it was no use. He saw Ivar bend over and bite Erik, coming back up with a full mouth of flesh. Erik stopped moving.

"No!" Aedan screamed. A tear ran down his cheek as he watched his blood-brother's still body. Ivar managed to get the seax out of his foot and was running toward the boat. Nine other former crewmen joined him, also now draugar. The group groaned and reached for the boat, but seemed unable to enter the water.

Aedan watched the corpse from the mound stand calmly on the strand. He didn't struggle to the surf. He simply watched the boat pull away from the shore, standing tall and menacing.

He slumped down and cried as the remaining crew rowed the *Ottar* away from shore.

What felt like hours later, Aedan woke, hoping he had been having a nightmare. He glanced around the deck of the *Ottar*, but Erik was nowhere to be seen.

The crew that remained looked ill. He saw them lying between the benches clutching their stomachs. He also saw that Draugr's Bane was glowing faintly. His blood went icy cold as he listened. He pulled out his Mjolnir pendant from beneath his tunic and held it between his thumb and forefinger. He prayed to Thor, the strongest of the gods. His Irish ancestors had also prayed to many gods before the White Christ. He thought he remembered one named Lugh, but no matter. Thor was his god now. He hoped Thor would come and smite these evil creatures.

His mind raced and he thought about what might happen if these beasts made it back to the Northlands. Gods, they would all become draugar. Aedan had to do something.

He couldn't kill them all, especially in these confined quarters. He could burn them, but then the boat would burn too, and that would leave him swimming at sea. The fire seemed to have no effect on them anyway. They didn't like the sea though, he thought. He would have to burn the boat, he could see no other way to keep them from his adopted homeland.

Aedan crept over to the mast and the brazier. He watched the men around him as he lit a fire and put on a pot, as if to boil water. He also took some straw used for bedding, and some fat for cooking, and dropped bits of it around the boat as he walked among the men. Draugr's Bane glowed more brightly now, and he could see the men looking sicker, their stench more foul by the minute. Aedan stuffed bits of oily cloth up his nose to mask the foul odor.

Once he reckoned he was ready, he kicked over the brazier and the hot coals scattered over the deck. The bits of straw and fat caught fire immediately. Aedan was shocked at how fast the blaze spread.

Men began moaning but they were too sick to get up and deal with the fire.

Aedan leaped over the benches to the stern of the boat, where the steering-oar was lashed. It was a massive piece of wood, much larger than a rowing oar. It might just be enough to allow Aedan to float on, like a small raft. He just had to get it loose from the ship.

The steering oar had a great deal of rope and leather holding it fast. He began hacking at the ropes and leather with his long-seax. Several of the outer strands split with little trouble, but the inner, more compressed rope, took longer. All the while, the fire spread rapidly fore and aft.

He heard one of the draugar making its way toward him, and saw its head poke up above the steering platform.

Aedan stood up straight and swung at the fiend's head. It was in a perfect position to be decapitated. Off went the head, and Aedan returned to hacking at the last two strands of iron-like rope.

Most of the draugar were on fire now, and the ship was fully ablaze. Aedan's cheeks stung from the heat.

Another draugr began clambering to the steering platform.

Aedan had to focus on the last rope. He had to get that cut before the ship went down, otherwise, he would be burnt alive, or drown.

The draugr stood up on the stern to its fully ghastly height, a drooling smile on its face.

He was momentarily paralyzed at the sight of the creature, then noticed the draugr was standing with its back toward the starboard the edge of the ship—only a few hand-widths above its heels.

Aedan ran forward with a kick, tripping the draugr backwards over the side. It plummeted beneath the waves.

He gave one last hack to the ropes and watched as the steering oar slipped quietly into the dark water. The fire was now an inferno; his cheeks blistered. He sheathed his long-seax and leaped, plunging into the freezing sea. He sank deep and fast, as though Aegir's daughters were pulling him down. Then his descent into the inky dark slowed. So deep was he, that Aedan could barely see light from the blaze above him now. He kicked and swam for his life.

His lungs near to bursting, he rose, almost mesmerized by the fire above him. Its light flickered and danced. It was beautiful, he thought. He broke the water gasping, his lungs burning as fiercely as the *Ottar*. He had never needed air so much, but after the heat of the fire, the sea was like ice.

He tread water as he scanned for the steering oar. There! It bobbed several ship-lengths astern of the *Ottar*. He swam desperately toward his last chance for life. He scrambled and clawed himself on top, then promptly collapsed. He had just enough strength to roll over and face the inferno. Northmen dreamt of a burial at sea in a burning ship; these men got better than his blood-brother. He lay his head down holding the edges of the steering oar as it rolled with the waves.

* * * *

Aedan lifted his head when he thought he heard voices, but knew he must be imagining them, as all the crew were either burned or drowned.

"You there!" a voice shouted.

That was no imagined call. He scanned around himself as the waves crested and fell. Under the flickering light of the burning ship, he spied the dragon headed prow of another longship. His chilled body flooded with the warmth of hope.

"Here!" he called, waving an arm, careful not to allow the steering-oar slip from beneath him, for he was too weary to swim.

Strong arms plucked him from the sea and wrapped him in a sour smelling bearskin.

"What happened to your ship, boy?" a man asked.

"It's a tale you'd scarce believe," Aedan answered honestly. His hand slid to the hilt of Draugr's Bane, reassuring himself that his prize remained safe.

"I look forward to hearing it then. We'll beach the ship and you can tell me all about . . ."

"No!" Aedan shouted. "Do *not* make landfall there, keep sailing!"

The men looked at him in astonishment. "Just give me a drink first, for gods' sake, and I'll tell you my tale."

Eye

May 1915

Three trolls shared an eye,
each with a hollow socket
in the middle of his forehead.
The one who had the eye
would go first, pounding
through the forest, the others
blundering behind. If the first one
grew weary, or they fought about
which way to go, he would pop out
the eye and give it to the next one.
Trolls think slow thoughts
like rocks. They take what
doesn't belong to them: coins, eggs,
girls for wives, boys for supper.

On the way to confirmation lessons,
cousin Ingerid and I stopped at Fjeldskleiv,
where the river tipped and dropped
to the town and church below. As
our mothers had instructed, we'd change
our carved tree-shoes for our only
leather pairs. In the middle of the river
was a troll kettle, a deep bowl in the rock
where trolls come to boil their dinner.
Ingerid and I hooked our shoes quickly,
always looking over our shoulders.

One day, something came over me,
recklessness or haughtiness,
and I climbed down to the kettle, sat
on its rim, dangled my bare feet

inside. Shadows bent over the water.
Ingerid screamed, "Come away!"
I smiled, and she screamed
again, ran down the steep hill.

The river grew loud in the silence
left behind, and I sat quiet, my feet
swirled by the eddy. I sat a long time,
sound washing over my body,
shadows lengthening toward me.

By Linda Strever

The Good, the Evil, and the Ugly

Saroj Chumber

She stared at her reflection in the mirror. Her red dress reached just below her knees draping itself around her well-shaped figure, the neckline plunging deeply enough to promise heaven. She applied lipstick to her full lips, blonde curls dancing around her face as she moved her hands. The bracelets on her wrist clinked as she finished and gave a last satisfied look in the mirror. She could hear laughter and songs. The bar was filled with mountain trekkers and tourists. She always tried to pick them carefully. The trick was to find someone who would not be easily missed. She had discovered how easy it was to get a man to open up after a couple of beers. The dress and the cleavage did the rest. With a smile, she left her house.

* * * *

Scott Williams stared at his watch. The night was getting dark and the clientele in the bar more boisterous. He looked around, noting the décor, heavy on the wood and the wine-red drapes that framed the windows; typical Norwegian style, built like a tavern from the Middle Ages, with tables and benches hewn from long wooden logs. He wondered if this is where Diego had also sat. It had been several months since he had gone missing without a trace. The Norwegian police had closed the case for lack of evidence. Diego had simply vanished. They suspected he might have fallen into one of the lakes.

But Scott saw him in his dreams, and the dreams had gotten more and more vivid. It was nearly the same each time. Diego's pale face seemed to peep from a narrow waterway, and his voice called out, but Scott could never make sense of the words. Boulder or builder, or something. It made no sense. In the vision, Scott saw tall dark trees with moss all round. Was he under a boulder in the woods? The trees were so dense, sunlight struggled to find the ground.

Scott would wake up, sweating. They were like brothers and the fact that they shared a birthday made that bond even stronger. When Diego went missing, he was sure it was nothing and that he would show up, suddenly. Diego was known to take long exotic vacations. Scott twirled his glass. The liquor was strong but he was still in control. It was past midnight and he was feeling tired. The girl serving drinks at the bar smiled at him.

"Your first time here?"

"How could you tell?

"You have tourist eyes," she said and laughed. Her eyes were large and brown, with thick eyelashes that fanned her cheeks when she looked down. She was beautiful.

"What brings you here?"

"The same as others." He smiled, wondering if she could read his mind. She must be used to men staring at her.

"It can't be the mountains. You seem to be searching for someone. I was watching you. You were sizing up everyone in the place."

"You missed your calling. You should have been a detective!" He was almost slurring.

"I think you're ready to call it a night."

"I'm looking for a friend. He came here last year and simply disappeared. The police have no leads and the trails end here. This is where he was last seen."

"A close friend?"

"Yeah, we're like brothers."

She seemed a bit pensive, then decided to speak. "Perhaps he was taken."

"Taken? By what?"

"I don't know, really. A mysterious spirit? But your friend is not the only one missing. A couple of years back a woman came searching for her husband. They never found him and later she went missing too."

"Spooky. But it makes me even more determined to find him. "

"If the police have no trace of him . . . I would just give up."

"I can't."

Scott ordered another drink. Twenty minutes later he left the bar and began the long walk to his small hotel. The road was dark and dimly lit. He felt himself swaying and regretted many of the shots. That was some strong stuff. As he made his way along the road, he could see someone in the distance. A woman. A beautiful woman in a red dress, sitting on a milestone marker by the side of the road. Even before his alcohol-infused brain could function, the woman smiled, waved towards him, motioning him to come to her.

"Hello, stranger." Her voice was soft as silk. "I'm in trouble. Can you please help?"

"Of course." Scott swayed slightly but he was ever the Gentleman.

"My house is close, but I twisted my ankle. Can you help me get home?"

"Sure, but how? Piggyback?" The words slipped out with a snort of laughter.

"That might work. I'm not so heavy." She smiled then winced as she tried to stand up.

Her ankle might be swollen, but he was not sure as his eyes were blurred.

He helped her up and hoisted her onto his back. She curled her arms around him, and pointed towards a distant light.

"I live there, in my cottage."

He nodded and resolved to fight the drunkenness that made him unsteady. She was a feather and it was no problem to carry her on his back.

"My name is Hilde."

"I'm Scott."

By the time they reached her cottage, he had sobered up somewhat. He put her down by the front door. In the light of the cottage he had a proper look at his passenger. She was breathtakingly beautiful, smiling at him with obvious interest.

"Please, will you carry me to my bed?" He nodded.

Inside, Scott carried her to the back; the bedroom. Her bed was covered with a lamb's wool blanket. He removed it and placed her gently down on the mattress. She looked up at him. He could not resist.

* * * *

Despite their different backgrounds, Scott stayed in Hilde's cottage. He had fallen in love before but this was different. His feelings for her defied all logic. He quit his job and started working on her little farm. Hilde was mysterious and was given to sudden disappearances but she was usually quite happy, performing her daily chores, making butter, tending to her animals. Scott never saw her naked. She was always wearing long skirts. One day as she was cooking in the kitchen, he crept up from behind and laid a hand on her behind. She jumped as if electrocuted.

"Don't sneak up on me like that!"

"What is that under your skirt, Hilde. I felt something."

"Nothing. It must be my dress that has bunched up." She seemed eager to change the subject.

"Let me see." He reached for her, but she slapped his hand away immediately.

"Don't touch me there!"

Shocked he stared at her. "Why not?"

"Just don't!" She ran out before he could say anything more.

Confused, he sat down on the rocking chair in the living room and waited for her to come back. Eventually, he got worried and went looking for her. He walked far into the woods that surrounded her farm, but found no trace of her anywhere. After many hours, he headed back. She was home, waiting for him, smiling her enticing smile. He was so relieved to see her that he forgot all about the strange episode.

* * * *

A few months later, she came to him and told him her news. "I'm going to have a baby!"

Scott was overjoyed. He went and plucked apples and they baked a pie to celebrate. He told her he must call his mother and let her know. Hilde's expression grew serious. It was the first time he had mentioned his other life in all the time they had been together. He seemed to be happy, living with her, almost cut-off from the rest of the world. His mother was very happy to hear from him.

"Scott, what have you been up to? How could you quit your job and just move abroad?"

"Mother, I'll tell you everything! But first, the good news. You're going to be a grandmother!"

"When will I meet this mysterious woman of yours? She seems to have bewitched you. You have forgotten everyone. I am not so sure I like that, Scott."

* * * *

It was a stormy night when their daughter came into the world. Hilde did not cry or scream as Scott had heard women do when giving birth. Instead, she sang and danced in the rain. Scott thought she had gone crazy and pleaded with her to stay indoors, but she laughed and carried on dancing, her big belly swaying. When she had danced for what seemed like hours, she came in, soaked to her skin, her eyes gleaming and a big smile on her face. She asked Scott to fetch clean towels and she lay down on the floor. Then she let out a long wail. At the end of it, their child was born. Scott was overwhelmed, as he held his daughter for the first time. Then he noticed something. He turned the baby and saw it. A small tail protruding from her back, like a goat's.

Hilde saw his shocked look and took his hand. "Don't worry Scott. She is like me. She is a Hulder."

He felt his head swim and he wondered if he was dreaming. That was the day she showed him her own tail. He finally saw it, the hollow in her back and the little tail hanging between her legs. It felt unreal but when he touched it, he knew it was a part of her. She was Hulder, the witch. He was silent for days, not knowing how to deal with the strangeness of the situation. But he loved her. He stayed. She sang and bathed the baby and he helped. She called their daughter Elina.

* * * *

He had come to terms with living with a Hulder. Their baby was now six months old. One day a couple of trees near Hilde's farm fell, after a storm. Scott went to clear the area of the great trunks and torn out roots. That is when he saw it; a hand, almost skeletonized, but unmistakably human. He dug around the trees and to his shock discovered many more skeletons. When he confronted her that day, she confessed. There were many men she had seduced and the ones who had displeased her had met with death. She had buried them amongst the trees. Diego was also there, in the small creek near her farm.

"All this time . . . all this time, you knew I was searching for him. What kind of a woman could do this?" Scott could barely utter the words. His face distorted in disbelief. He marvelled at Hilde's composure. She seemed unmoved.

"How many men are we talking about here?"

"Many." She almost smiled.

"Do you feel no guilt? Or remorse?"

"Remorse? Guilt? Those are not words I am familiar with." She replied calmly. "Can you ask a lion why it eats a lamb? I am not human, Scott."

"Then why did you spare me?"

"I have no answer to that except that you please me. It is the closest I can come to feeling love." She smiled, then continued. "It's my tail. It makes me do crazy things. I lose control."

"What if you get rid of it? What will happen, then?"

"I will not be me, anymore. I will become good and kind."

"Then I want you to get rid of your tail."

"Ah, so typical. Commit to a man and he asks you to do the unthinkable for him. What if I change into someone else? Will you still love me?"

"Yes, I will always love you, Hilde. I left everything for you. Surely, it is not a big sacrifice on your part to give up a tail that only makes you do evil."

"Alright." She got up and fetched a knife. "You promise to love and cherish me in all my forms?"

"I do."

With one stroke, she chopped off the tail. She screamed and for the first time Scott saw her cry. Blood splattered the floor, pumped from the wound on her back. She threw the amputated appendage to the ground, sobbing. The tail twitched, as if grieving to be separated from her, before it became still. A small flame sparked upon it, and soon there were just ashes. Scott's gaze was drawn to the burning flesh. He turned to thank her, but she was gone. Instead, a very ugly woman stood before him. Her face was creased in wrinkles and she had large warts over her hands and chin.

"Who are you?" Scott screamed. "Where is Hilde?"

"I am Hilde," the ugly woman replied sadly, and Scott knew it was so.

"You see, Scott, the tail made me bad but it also made me beautiful."

"Why didn't you tell me what would happen if you cut your tail?" he moaned.

"Would it have mattered?"

Scott did not reply.

* * * *

Scott tried to love her but he could not forget his beautiful Hilde. This ugly creature lying next to him in bed was a stranger. He wept for the woman he loved. After a few weeks, he knew he had to leave. He wanted to go back to his life in England and to reality.

When he told her, Hilde was strangely quiet. She watched him pack his bags, silently. When he came to bid her adieu, she finally spoke.

"My mother did the same for my father. He begged her to chop off her tail. Then he left her because she was no longer beautiful. She warned me never to be mad enough to lose my tail over any man. But this strange thing you call 'love,' this made me believe that what we had was real."

"I am truly sorry, Hilde. It is not just what you look like but also what you did. You killed my best friend. It's just too much."

"If I was still beautiful, I am sure you would not have cared." Elina, their child, crawled towards her mother, her tail swishing back and forth. Hilde picked up the baby.

"You'll never cut your tail, my little one. Never."

Pesta

She's walked this world—Both far and back.
Her soul, what's left, has turned jet black.
Black as the cloak she hides within,
Black as the recess of the Brown Bear's den.
Depending on what you see in her hand,
You can sense The Maker's Plan.
If you see the old crone's rake,
She's taken pity for your sake.
Of your family a few will live.
Take the gift she offers to give.
For if it's Pesta's broom you see,
Death will come quickly for you and me.

By Kally Jo Surbeck

And The Snow Came Down

Andrew James Murray

Torsten Göransson bid the widow Berget farewell one last time, before stepping out into the cold winter night. He paused to survey the scene, pulling his collar tight. It had been snowing a little when he had crossed Anna's threshold, an hour before, but now the snow was coming down harder, the wind getting up. His boot prints leading here were almost covered, and soon there would be no trace of his pastoral visit. He squinted myopically against the flakes driven into his face, but his gaze was turned inward.

He felt finally that he was gaining some acceptance among the people here, Anna Berget being a case in point. When he had initially arrived in Fåberg two years ago, as the village's Lutheran pastor, he had received what could be described as a warm welcome from no one. In addition to suspicion, and sometimes barely concealed hostility, the closest thing to a welcome he had received was indifference. Was this the usual way Norwegian folk treated newcomers, or was it like this only in Oppland? The language had not been a barrier. Rather it was the twin facts of him being both a foreigner, as well as a city man. Not only was he from Sweden, but he was from Stockholm, and so was considered too far removed from the everyday rural life of this community to understand their ways. To be one of *them*.

And it was the village elders who had seemed the most resistant to his attempts to build bridges. Every time he had crossed paths with Anna, he would greet her warmly, only to receive a curt greeting or vapid smile in return. He would pause on seeing her approach on the path, waiting to exchange pleasantries, but she would continue past without even breaking stride. Of course, like everyone else, she would attend church, but she was reluctant to speak after the service. Just the same two words on the way out, "Pastor Göransson," with a slight nod of the head. Her attitude mirrored that of her neighbours. But, eventually, as happened with many of them, it was the younger generation that provided the breakthrough. Or rather, the breaking down of the walls that had been constructed, intentionally or not.

Children do not have the inhibitions of their parents and grandparents. They are inquisitive and innocent, more likely to engage. And being a witness to their exchanges and laughter causes infection: the warmth of the children's affections spread throughout each household. Soon a mother would add a line or two to a daughter's innocent jest, a father a rejoinder to a son's daring remark.

With Anna, it was her daughter Brigitta. Whenever she saw Torsten, she would ask him questions about his native Sweden, wanting to know *everything* about the country. Each answer he gave would barely be out of his mouth before the next question came, leading on from the previous one. Sometimes Anna would have to intervene if a question was deemed inappropriate, or too personal. Eventually Torsten spied a smile reluctantly forming on the edge of Anna's lips, as she would shepherd her daughter away. From that initial thawing, came visits such as the one tonight, where he would be welcomed into the home. She would never fully relax, he being an educated churchman, of course, but she was genial enough and it was progress.

And the same thing was happening throughout Fåberg. Families were accepting him, welcoming him, confiding in him. God be praised!

Torsten stooped slightly, bowing his head against the icy wind assailing him, and set off, his feet sinking into snow several inches deep. This was just the start, the advance guard of the season that would soon come roaring in from the north. Some of the older ones would not survive. Regrettable, but that is the way of things.

Thankful of that last glass of aquavit that Anna insisted he have to fortify against the cold, he made his way towards home, passing Dagnar Thorstad's place, which was the last before the church. Beyond the churchyard was his dwelling, at the edge of the village. Ideal for an outsider he supposed, with a rueful smile. He paused to look up at the church, his *true* home. This night it loomed over him, breaking through shadow and storm, standing resolute against the assault of time and tempest.

> *As long as the earth endures,*
> *sowing and reaping,*
> *cold and heat,*
> *summer and winter,*
> *day and night*
> *shall cease no more.*

Snowdrift was beginning to layer against the door, and Torsten sighed in the knowledge that it would have to be cleared in the morning. A sudden shiver swept through him; ice spreading through his veins. He pulled his hat lower so the brim rested just above his eyes, another stanza coming to mind.

The storm wind comes from the Mansion of the South,

and the North winds usher in the cold.

God breathes, and the ice is there,

the surface of the waters freezes over.

The way of things. Nature had a way of reminding of the consistency of God's laws. The village was now covered by an immaculate shroud, no building exempt from the sacred transformation.

Torsten turned for home, a lone traveller outside tonight. He had only gone a few yards when he stopped. He peered into the darkness beyond the village border, thinking he had heard something other than the storm. No, there was nothing. Just the gust of the biting wind or maybe the creaking of tree branches beneath their mantle of snow.

He continued a few more steps then halted. There it was again. Something above the wind, carried, but then snatched away, before he could fully grasp it. He peered into the darkness, blinking as the snow blurred his eyes, his reddened cheeks stinging.

What was it? It was high pitched, short in length. All he could see was the outline of the forest, the tall spruce barely discernible in the all-blanketing white.

There! Again! Definitely something other than the element's hymn to life. He walked a few paces in the direction of the forest, his feet sinking deeper in the snow. It couldn't be the animals over on the Andersen farmstead, it was too far away, and the wind wasn't coming from that direction.

Torsten stood a few moments, straining his ears, indecisive, about to turn back, when he noticed the snow in front of him begin to swirl in a circle, round and round like autumn leaves, caught in a draught. For a few seconds more it spun, then the twisting gyre lifted, moving contrary to the direction of the wind. He watched, puzzled, as phrases like *cross-winds,* and, implausibly, *sandstorms,* passed fleetingly through his mind, until, still unable to fathom what he was seeing, the circle moved rapidly away from him, ploughing a furrow through the snow towards the trees. A path was being created *against* the wind and the driving snowfall, of its own volition.

Torsten, unable to help himself, took a hesitant step into the furrowed tunnel, then another, and began to walk along the path away from the village. Narrowing his eyes, he could make out that the path, the furrow, had stopped moving, coming to rest at the dark base of a tree.

And then that sound again. It was definitely a cry that he could hear. He began to walk faster, and faster, the cold suddenly forgotten, barely resisting the urge to run along the channel towards the sound, towards the tree. Then, as he got closer, he could see something. Something other than the tree. A small dark shape, where the path ended. Torsten approached, and as the form came into focus, a small gasp escaped him as he stood over it, eyes wide.

A baby! My God, a baby! It was undeniably a baby, wrapped in a blanket and just left to die of exposure. Who would do such a thing? It must have only just been abandoned, as the swaddled child would surely have been covered by the snow. How long would it take to freeze to death out here on a night such as this?

He bent and picked up the bundle. Was the baby alive? It was hard to tell in these shadows-its eyes were scrunched shut, unmoving, only the tiny face visible. But he had heard a cry. Time was of the essence! If the baby was to have any chance of survival then he had to get it indoors fast. He pulled the edge of the blanket tightly around the young one's face, then turned and broke into a run, back along the furrow, towards the village. The village—who could it be? Who in the village was pregnant, or had a young baby? Just as quickly as the questions came, he pushed them away. Along with the barely entertained observation that there had been no tracks or footprints around it at all. There was time for all that later.

He reached the end of the furrowed path, where the cycle of snow had first started to move before his uncomprehending eyes, and then his gait slowed as he started to move through the deeper snow beyond the path. He held the baby tight to his chest, willing what bodily heat he had to pass through into the infant.

It was cold, freezing; this little one's life was in his hands. They were both in God's hands.

Christ be with me, he muttered audibly. *Christ be with me.*

He stumbled, slipping in the snow, putting one hand out to stop himself falling, his other hand clutching the little one. He gasped for breath as the gale began to howl behind him, buffeting him as he lumbered along. Now more than ever, he felt he was doing God's work. A great responsibility fell upon him, a sense that everything hung upon how he acted, right here, right now. On this night would he be judged.

On he went, ploughing through the snow that was beginning to drift higher, as he retraced his steps. He slipped again, going down fully this time. But he did not let go of the infant. He looked up and saw the churchyard, the headstones, like malformed teeth. He was nearly there, nearly home. Slowly rising to his knees, he looked down to make sure he had protected the baby in the fall. He froze.

To his senses, it was as if the wind had ceased, the snow had stopped falling, the cold had left him. It was as if everything else had ceased to exist and it was just he and the baby, protected and sheltered in a private, solitary place.

Except it wasn't a baby.

The woollen blanket was now little more than a bundle of dirty, torn rags, frozen stiff and unyielding with ice. And the baby . . . the baby! There was a skull where before there had been a face. Dirty, fragile, aged. A couple of other, small, thin bones protruded from the rags.

He was clutching a parcel of frozen bones.

He shook his head, trying to make the vision alter, thinking of the cold air and Anna Berget's aquavit. But the terrible sight remained. Terror, confusion, denial, all battled for supremacy as he moved to throw the cold, moldered remains down, only to find that he couldn't. His hands were frozen, his arms immobile. And that sense of responsibility that he had felt, that imperative compulsion to act, *increased,* as though this *still* was the moment where everything was to be decided.

He knew that this feeling did not emanate from God. It was coming from something else. He stared at the fleshless face, at the tiny, eyeless sockets, and a word began to form in his mind, that part of his mind that still attempted to rationalise it all. An improbable word. An impossible word, a word that he had heard once mentioned by an old, superstitious villager that had brought derisory laughter from his two sons.

Myling.

At the very moment his fumbling mind latched onto that word, the sense of protected isolation shattered and the wind struck him more forcefully than ever, as he sank to his knees. The wind raged and the darkness threatened to swallow him.

Myling.

Despite the intense, numbness enveloping him, the word spread a different kind of cold throughout his entire being. A cold that was driving out everything else. He knew how easy it would be to succumb, to lie here and be buried with this . . . thing.

Pushing that thought away, he rose on unsteady legs and began to move forward, clutching the collection of rags and bones so tightly he thought they would break. He pushed himself on, feeling his life imperilled. That responsibility he had felt to act was now something *more,* it was a great weight bearing down upon him, increasing all the time, as Torsten, gripped with an unholy terror, battled forward, against the snow, against the wind, against the weight and fear.

He battled for his soul, and that of the child's.

He reached the churchyard edge and turned towards his house, but was consumed by the hissing roar of a thousand angry cats, clawing at him from the inside. He shot back instinctively towards the churchyard, and the cats were silenced. On some intuitive level, he knew what was expected of him, and what he must do, and the price that would be exacted if he failed.

He fell against the churchyard gate. It refused to budge, heavy and resisting, frozen shut. Torsten threw his shoulder against it once, twice, and it swung open, as he fell inside the church grounds. He crawled, clutching the thing, the baby, the bones, whose spiralling weight was now too much and pressed him down, preventing him from standing. He inched his way forward, across the buried stone path. At some point he had lost his hat, and his hair hung lank against the sides of his face. With his last ounce of strength, he came to his knees, and despaired.

The ground was covered by a foot of snow. And even if he managed to clear some away, the earth beneath would be as hard as iron. He would never be able to do it. Waves of fear and failure passed over him as the hissing returned, more urgent now than before. But with the sense of failure, he refused acceptance.

Torsten closed his eyes, hunching over as he rocked the baby, a parody of a doting father. Trying to block everything out, he turned inward, to his sanctuary; that landscape of prayer, housed within his heart, that was exempt from all except God. He fell back on his faith, not the last desperate action of a drowning man, but the action of a righteous man who refuses to doubt. He cried out *"As God is my witness, I promise that I will give this child a proper Christian burial! Somewhere within this hallowed ground, as befits all children of God!"*

The wind took the words, accepting the conviction behind them. The hissing once more silenced, and the impossible weight lifted, the sense of danger falling away. The bundle fell from Torsten's hands, rolling in the snow to lie at his side as he, too, fell. He lay on his back, motionless, weeping, looking up at the church framed against the consoling sky.

The snow came down harder than ever, and with it, by God's grace, a sense of peace.

Slipping

Slipping –
With nothing to hold onto
Uprooted roots –
Slick ropes –
Dash my hopes
After the long fall
I feel so small
When I lay shattered.
But I do not bruise
When I am battered
If I could just muster
A passable smile, a laugh –
You'd never know
It would never, ever show.
Sometimes I can pull it off
Put it up –
Pretend life is a silver cup
But the mask –
It never lasts
In the end
It's always –
Slipping

By Sasha Kasoff

The Yule Chair

April 1917

In the old days
they set out great carved bowls
for Christmas Eve:
one with water,
one with milk,
one with ale,
one with brandy.

They took their best clothes,
hung them over the chairs,
and walked around the table
three times.

They sat down in the chairs
and went to sleep, their heads
nestled in their arms.
The unmarried ones dreamed.

The one who came first
into the dream you would marry.
If this man or this woman
drank of the brandy,
you would be rich.
If it was the ale,
you would be lucky.
If it was the milk,
you would be unlucky.
If it was the water,
you would be

very poor.

This is the way
Mama first saw Papa.
She never told us
from which bowl
he drank.

By Linda Strever

Between Two Worlds

Claire Casey

Walking through the museum one last time before her shift ended, Kilda was never surprised to find visitors still in the building after they had shut for the night. It never mattered how often people were told the museum was closing, there were always those who continued on, regardless. It was made more difficult when she had to deal with those who huffed and puffed, as they complained under their breath, all while being guided out of the building. Kilda had noticed that a number of people had come to the museum, to visit the temporary exhibition on local folklore. It had opened a few days before, and was certainly proving popular. Glancing at the glass cabinets as she passed, Kilda was amused by what people had once believed. Her own grandmother was a clear example of a superstitious islander.

That evening everything was quiet; no one to deal with. All the displays were as they should be. Finishing her rounds, Kilda went to the staff room. She pulled on her long, wool coat and grabbed her bag before she made her way to the front door. Stepping out into the cold winter evening, she locked up and walked through the courtyard, which led to the main street that snaked its way through Kirkwall. She could see other people heading home from work, or making their way to the nearest pub for a quick pint. Despite the chill in the air, she enjoyed the evenings, when she had the chance to go for a long walk. There was something about the sharpness of the cold that made her feel alive.

A group of young women walked in front of her, heading in the same direction. They were laughing loudly, enjoying each other's company. So much so, they did not notice that one of them had dropped something. Quickening her pace, Kilda picked it up. It was a purse. Not something anyone would want to lose, least of all on a night out. Calling after them, she returned it to its owner, allowing Kilda to continue on her way, while the women continued on theirs.

Looking up at the sky, she marvelled at the gleaming stars. She was never alone when she could see their light. Kilda walked past the cathedral and hurried on her way to the bay. She didn't feel like she belonged in Kirkwall, even though she had lived in the town her whole life. Her family had lived in Orkney for generations, but knowing this only added to her feeling of restlessness. The open ocean was there to remind her of all the adventures she was missing. She had always been drawn to the water's edge, no matter what the weather decided to throw at her, and she felt most at home looking into its dark depths.

She was only twenty-seven and she felt that life was passing her by. Whatever it was she was meant to be doing always seemed to lie just beyond the furthest horizon, just beyond her grasp. She often wondered what life would be like if she packed up everything she owned and disappeared to wherever fate took her. Feeling the salt-laden breeze against her face, she smiled as the bay came into view. She followed the road around to the quieter part, which took her away from the harbour. Kilda loved how the lights of Kirkwall danced across the surface of the water. There was something magical about the sight.

She stopped and took a deep breath, allowing her mind to wander. There was no one else about, even though the pubs and restaurants at the harbour were filled to bursting. Most people she knew tended to prefer the company of others, but Kilda had always preferred to be alone. These moments of solitude gave her the time she needed to think. It wasn't as if she thought about anything in particular, she just enjoyed being able to lose herself in her imagination.

That was until she saw something, out in the water of the bay. Looking closely she could just make out a man swimming in the sea. Kilda was certain that the water was freezing cold, especially at that time of year. Stepping off the pavement, she made her way across the narrow beach. Stopping at the water's edge, she saw something draped over a nearby rock. She picked it up, only to realise she was holding a sealskin.

Her first reaction was to throw the thing down at her feet, but something stopped her. Pulling her bag off her shoulder, she quickly stuffed the skin inside. She looked back at where she had seen the man, but he was no longer there. Glancing around the bay, she started to panic. Had he drowned right in front of her? Kilda had no idea what to do now.

"Good evening, my lady" a voice said from behind her.

She let out a shriek and spun around coming face to face with a man. A naked man, dripping wet, with black, shoulder length, slicked back hair. Kilda found she couldn't help but look at what stood before her. He had the build of an Olympic swimmer, with a mix of strength and grace in even the slightest movement. The gentleness mixed with playfulness in his gaze was alluring, and she found herself drawn to him.

"Has no one ever told you not to creep up on someone like that?" Kilda stated, harsher than she had intended.

"I am sorry if I alarmed you," he said. "That was not my intention. As you can see, I am in a difficult situation." He gave her the slightest of bows.

"I can see that. You must be frozen. What the hell were you doing swimming in the bay? Where are your clothes?" Kilda did all she could to keep eye contact.

"I always find that swimming in the sea to be highly refreshing. I believe that someone must have taken my clothes while I was in the water, leaving me like this. Would you be kind enough to help me?"

"I can't really leave you standing out here like that. You could come to my house. I'll be able to sort something out for you, once we get there." She frowned. "But how to get you there in the first place? Seeing you like that will probably give my neighbours a heart attack." Kilda racked her brain for ideas.

"And what may I call you?" he asked, with a smile. "I must know the name of the woman who came to my aid."

"My name's Kilda. As in the island. My parents thought it sounded pretty. What about you?"

"I am Erlend. I will be forever in your debt if you help me and I will do all that I can to repay you," he replied.

Kilda felt herself beginning to blush at the old-fashioned charm of the man. She tried not to act like a shy schoolgirl, as a plan began to form in her mind. Her house wasn't that far from the bay and she knew it wouldn't take long for them to get there. Taking off her coat, she managed to get Erlend to wrap it around himself. It was clearly too small for him, but covered at least some of his nakedness. It would have to do. Signalling for him to follow, they made their way through the back streets. Kilda became aware that he was studying everything. It was as if he was seeing things with new eyes. Things that Kilda took for granted, from street lighting to cars, but Erlend would stop in his tracks, examining everything. After much coaxing, they arrived at her front door. She slipped the key into the lock. The door opened directly into the front room of the house, allowing them to step directly into the heart of her home.

"Welcome to my humble abode. It isn't anything fancy, but it's home." The furniture and décor was basic, but it was warm and clean.

"I can assure you that your home is very welcoming. Just like your good self," Erlend replied with a warm smile.

"Thank you." Kilda felt herself blushing again.

"There is no need for you to thank me. I should be the one thanking you."

"Right, I should really get you some clothes, before you catch your death of cold." She turned and made her way into her bedroom.

What was coming over her? She kept telling herself that she did not know this man who had just walked into her life. Yet she couldn't help falling for him. Part of her feared that as soon as she helped him, he would walk out the front door. But he had every right to leave once she had helped him. She was nothing to him but a good Samaritan, and it would be natural for them to go their separate way, sooner than later. But she hoped that he would stay. Putting those thoughts to the back of her mind, she threw her bag into a corner. She would deal with it as soon as she could.

Opening her wardrobe, she searched through everything. Her brother had left clothes and a pair of old boots with her the last time he visited. She had put them somewhere. She was certain that the old clothes would fit Erlend, as he was about the same height and build as her bother. Finding the clothes and boots, she grabbed hold of them and went back into the living room.

"Here you go. Hopefully these will do you. Are you staying nearby? Are you needing a hand getting there?" Kilda asked as she handed him the clothes.

"In all honesty, I am something of a wandering soul, with no fixed abode." Erlend replied as he pulled on the clothes.

"You mean you've been sleeping outside?"

"I have been sleeping wherever I can find a place to rest my head. It hasn't been that cold, I assure you. There's no need for you to worry about me."

"Either way, it isn't really the weather for sleeping rough. You can stay here until you find your own place, or you head off to wherever it is you're going."

"That is very kind of you. Would I not be a burden? Surely I would only be getting in your way?"

"I'm sure if you were ever to become a burden, I would let you know." Kilda told him, feeling herself drawn to him even more.

* * * *

Kilda lay in her bed, unable to sleep as she kept thinking over the day's events. It had started out quite normally, yet it ended with a naked homeless man sleeping in her house. Luckily, she didn't have to work the next day; she was going to be utterly exhausted. The thought of the sealskin had played on her mind. She could not stop herself from thinking about it. Why she had taken it? She knew, without question, that it was connected to Erlend. No matter what her suspicions, she could not ask him.

She was reminded of the stories her grandmother used to tell of the selkies and how they would come ashore in human form. Her grandmother had insisted that all of the creatures of myth existed and lived alongside humans, even though most people had lost the ability to see them. Even from a young age, Kilda knew that her parents did not approve of what her grandmother was telling her. There were whispers that her grandma had the Sight. She could remember believing she saw selkies whenever she saw seals on the shoreline. But she wasn't a child any longer.

She had long since put those stories behind her, but now, she wasn't sure what she believed. Finally slipping into sleep, Kilda dreamed of her grandma, and of seals who were really people, as well as people who were really seals.

Waking the next morning, Kilda found herself surprisingly fresh. Getting up, she quickly dressed, and made her way into the front room, where she discovered Erlend standing at the window, watching what was going on in the world beyond. He was already dressed, and seemed unaware of her presence. This allowed her to get a good look at him in the morning light. There was a grace about him that she found appealing. She smiled.

"I hope that you slept well last night. I would have offered you the spare room, but it's full of junk at the moment and missing a bed. So the sofa was really the only option," Kilda said.

Erlend turned to face her. "I did sleep well. I don't mind having to sleep on the sofa. Thank you for allowing me to stay."

"It was the least I could do. You must be hungry" Kilda answered, realising that she was feeling pangs herself.

"I am famished," he replied, with the flash of a smile.

"I know a brilliant place that's not far from here," Kilda told him as she turned and made her way back into her room. "Just give me a second."

Grabbing her bag, she opened it, only to see the sealskin was still there. Taking it out, she hid it under the bed, where it would be safe. For the time being at least. They left the house and made their way through Kirkwall, with Kilda leading, until they came to the Peel café. With breakfast ordered, they relaxed in each other's company. Later Kilda showed Erlend the town, allowing him to see all that Kirkwall had to offer. With the passing of the day, Kilda slowly began to forget the mystery of the sealskin.

* * * *

The months passed and Erlend still had not moved out. Instead, Kilda had found herself asking him to stay. He returned her affections, but she continued to make sure the sealskin was securely kept out of sight. She had acquired an old wooden strong box, which she could lock. She kept the key on her person. She would sometimes open the box and take the skin out. She would sit and hold it, feeling the texture of skin and fur as she turned it over it in her hands. She only ever did that when the house was empty and there was no chance of being discovered.

She still worked at the museum, but spent much of her spare time with Erlend. One night, as she lay in bed, she turned to Erlend, who was sleeping soundly at her side. She could no longer imagine life without him. She had something to say, but she struggled to find the right words, as well as the right moment. Many men would run at the slightest suggestion of . . . She would not be able to hide it for much longer. She rested her hands on her stomach. She didn't know if it was her imagination, but she was certain that it was already beginning to swell.

* * * *

The years came and went and Kilda allowed herself to enjoy the simple joys of watching Erlend as he played with their three young children. As so often, the family could be found playing on the beach. They had long since moved house, when their family began to grow, but they had only gone a couple of doors along the street. Despite the happiness she felt at watching her kids, she still felt there was something missing. Something was calling to her.

Even though she continued to keep the sealskin hidden from Erlend and from their children, there were still moments when she would sit and hold it. Erlend never asked, but she suspected he knew that she had it.

* * * *

Kilda stood on the beach, looking out to sea, the sealskin in her hands. A decade had passed since Erlend had come into her life. She could not stop thinking of that night, for all of the wrong reasons. It was the night the sealskin had come into her possession.

She was happy. Erlend was the love of her life. They had three beautiful children and she had a job she enjoyed, especially since being promoted to manager, which allowed her to bring about the changes in the museum she had always wanted. Yet, she wanted more. And that feeling was getting stronger.

She placed the skin on the ground at her feet. She slipped out of her clothes, which she folded and placed next to her bag, on the ground. Kicking off her shoes, she left them where they fell. Taking the sealskin in her hands, she pulled it onto her back. It was warm against her naked skin. She blinked in surprise. Her entire world had changed. Kilda could feel the beach under her sleek form as she began to pull herself towards the water's edge. She mourned what she had given up, but she continued to make her way into the sea. The water was not cold. It felt like home.

* * * *

Erlend left the house, a look of concern on his face. Kilda was never out this late when she went on one of her walks. If she was anywhere, she would be down at the beach, gazing out at the sea. The children were already in bed and fast asleep, but he couldn't rest until he knew Kilda was safe. The wind was cold on his face and he could smell rain in the air and he worried, because he knew that Kilda had not worn a coat.

Setting foot on the beach, he sensed that Kilda was not there. Then he saw a pile of clothes in the middle of the beach, with the incoming tide threatening to engulf them. He ran to them. He had known she had hidden the sealskin from him since their paths had crossed, ten years before. She had done all that she could to make sure that he never laid hands on it again. But that was okay. He didn't care. He loved her and wanted to spend the rest of his life with her. So much so, he had given up his former life. That had been the choice that he had made and he would do the same again. But knowing that Kilda had left him, he felt his heart breaking.

Burying his face in her clothes, he could smell her. He cried. He did not know if he would see her again. He could not bear to think about that. Not yet. He turned for the only home he had left. There were those who had to be told their mother was gone.

* * * *

It had been a year since Kilda had vanished. The whole town presumed that she must have killed herself, even though there was no body. There had been those who had claimed she had swum out into the bay and succumbed to exhaustion and cold, only for her body to be washed out to sea. Erlend alone understood the truth.

He stood, watching the children as they played on the beach, calling to each other. They had struggled to come to terms with the loss of their mother, but as with all children, they were resilient and were bouncing back. Watching them made him smile. They reminded him of happier times, when Kilda had made him feel as if he was the man she had always wanted. Now, he belonged more above the waves than he did below and there was no way for him to return. His children were here. He had never wanted them to know their father was a selkie who had lost his sealskin and become human. He had never wanted them to know their mother had taken his skin and had become a selkie.

Turning his attention away from his children, he looked out into the bay. A slight movement caught his eye. He could see a seal, but he knew that it was more than that. It remained where it was, its head just above the water as it watched the children as they chased the waves that rolled onto the beach. Erlend felt his breath catching in his throat. He wanted to call out, but he stopped himself, knowing it would never work.

The seal disappeared below the waves, leaving no trace it had ever been there. That didn't matter. He knew it was Kilda. He called the children. It was getting late. Time that they made their way home. Walking away from the beach, with the children in tow, his heart danced. Kilda had been watching. She was never far away, just out of sight. Maybe one day, she would come back? If she did, he would be waiting for her.

Visitation

My mother tells a story
told to her by her grandmother about her ancestors
(my ancestors), those clear-eyed Vikings
peeling back the skin of new worlds, soaking tangled
beards in honey mead, roaring at the sight of shore—No,
that is another story, although still hers (and mine).
This story is of humbler times spent hoeing parsnips
and rutabagas and whatever else would take root and grow
on windblown Danish fjords. And when the day unwrapped
its last buttery strands, the family—layered in wool and
stubborn earth—trudged back to their cobblestone
cottage (I am extrapolating here on likely construction
materials) that had sheltered countless generations of
Knudsens. They trudged back, heads down, path
memorized like drowsy bears lumbering to the
berry patch. (Wait, let's assume they had some joy
in their bony lives. These were sons and daughters of
Vikings, after all! They couldn't possibly have slipped
this far, I don't care how many centuries have
elapsed.) They sang that crazy song about the three little fish
dancing a jig under the ice as they tromped across the
lumpy landscape of salt-encrusted grasses (I am imagining
a sort of Scandinavian moor here) toward the warm
hearth and stewpot that awaited. Louie, always the loudest,
croaking like a jackdaw as each fish counted backwards
to the beginning of time. But no one gave a shit. Blood
is thicker than harmonics. And when these robust, turnip-fed
farmer Vikings shoved open the four-inch-thick
slab door (which was already slightly ajar) they gasped
and froze in their manured boots. An old woman
sat by the fire, stirring the stewpot, casting a wall-eyed
glance at the intruders. Eventually the family

began to thaw, mutter, shuffle cautiously along the edges
of the room. In time, the woman rose and
left, without a word spoken. Next week a cow died
and no one was surprised.

By Kim Goldberg

The Trolls of Stonehenge

Heather Norwood

Once upon a time, and likewise upon other times, the Vikings invaded that great land of Britain. Some Vikings sailed north, as Vikings are wont to do, and some sailed south. Those south-sailing ships were large and carried many people. However, when they arrived on the shores of the island, several women and children had disappeared. The Vikings, certain their ships contained murderous stowaways, disembarked, unloaded the cargo, and then set their ships out to sea. From the shore, they shot fiery arrows, and watched as their ships sank into the water.

The stowaways, Trolls who had boarded the ships in the wee hours, to escape being turned to stone by the Scandinavian sun, were borne away to this new land before the sun had set again. They had eaten their fill while on board, but then found themselves amidst several burning ships. They used their incredible strength to bash through the bottom of the ships and found themselves on the ocean floor.

It had taken the trolls several weeks to find the shore, and they were tired of eating fish, and holding their breath. They had set off in search of food or an unlikely bridge and found nothing. The sun cracked through the clouds of one grey dawn, and the trolls slowly solidified. Their feet became stuck, as though in mud, and were hardly moveable. They began to grunt and groan. It was not a new experience, this turning to stone, and yet they each struggled against it, every time. However, they were pleased to discover that if they willed it, after the sun had gone down for the night, they could reanimate. It was in this fashion that they traveled along the south of Britain, stone during the day, hungry trolls at night.

"I think we are lost," one of them said.

"I don't recognize any of this in the light," said another.

"Shh!" said several in tandem.

"Someone comes." They fell silent as their limbs froze, turned to rock.

A Viking child, covered in fur wet with melted snow and dark with dirt, approached the gigantic monoliths with awe. She took her hands out of a muff and placed both of her palms on one of the stones. The trolls watched with their invisible eyes as the girl walked in between and through the circle of stones they had created with their bodies. Their stomachs silently grumbled. It had been so long since they had eaten. They longed for the sensual ripping of skin, dripping of blood, that warm saltiness of the first bite that both ignites and dulls the senses. The longing grew more intense as the child began to dance and sing, her tiny body warming as she moved in the sun, a freshly-baked person.

A bell rang in the distance, and at long last the child left. In as much as stone can, the trolls relaxed. The sun was dipping low in the sky and they waited, patient, sleeping as snow fell across the plain. When the last ray of sunshine had fled, the trolls willed themselves to awaken.

"Which way did the child go?" one asked, shaking its enormous body free of paralysis, and bent its nose to the ground, like a dog.

In response, a few others grunted and pointed. Together, they moved slowly down the hill. With their great weight, they ambled, arms too heavy to swing, peering out from behind a blanket of matted hair, following a scent, leaving long gashes in freshly fallen snow with their bare feet. Smoke became visible in the moonlight, close, yet they did not reach the village in the glen until after the fires had gone out, the smoke dissipated.

"We don't have enough time to get a child," one said, staring out at the horizon, lit by the light of the moon on the white of the snow.

"There's sheep," said another.

Several grunted in assent, and they moved slowly towards a nearby pasture where a flock of sheep were grazing on grass poking out from the snow, unfazed by winter. The sheep and the trolls inhabited the same level of intelligence, even though one could speak, and the other only bleat. None of the sheep looked up as the trolls moved amongst them selecting choice cuts, but stepped aside to allow their passage.

When the shepherd Dagfin awoke in the morning, he noticed patches of red in the grass, and half of his flock missing. He rallied his sons Geert, Hektor and Mickel to organize a night watch. Armed with bows and arrows, they determined to rid their village of the menace that had cost them their sheep.

Dagfin and his boys sat cross-legged amongst the sheep wrapped in furs, passing a skin full of bitter ale. With each pass, their voices rose, until the skin was empty. Dagfin made the first run back to the house to refill the skin from the barrel. Each son in his turn made a trip back to the small wood cabin where their mother was sleeping soundly by the fire, unaware of their absence. Eventually, they built a fire against the cold and contented themselves with the watch, even though they had seen nothing at all that night. No sheep were lost, so they counted it a success. They agreed to do the same each night until they caught the predator.

For six nights, they sat and drank, and for six nights the village was safe. On the seventh morning, Dagfin and his sons were roused with aching heads from their slumber by a scream in the distance.

"Baaaa-beeette!" her mother screamed.

Geert was up the fastest and ran to Agnes, Babette's mother, to find out what happened. His attempt to calm her hysteria failed, and she was unable to say anything but her daughter's name over and over. Dagfin inspected the house and found that the child was gone and only urine spilled in fear was left in her wake.

The four men stood outside Agnes' house, and a knowing passed between them that went unspoken for the horror of it: whatever had eaten the sheep had taken poor Babette as well. It was then that, nodding to each other, they decided to tell the rest of the village about their sheep. They organized another watch, this time including all the men of the village who could shoot, and left their ale at home.

They decided to circle the village, unsure of the direction from which the threat might come. They walked slowly, quivers on their backs, bows in their hands. Light from the full moon aided their cause as they each scanned the distance expectantly. Hektor gasped when he saw them, coming from the north, and ran quietly to his brother. He elbowed Geert frantically and pointed to the large lumbering creatures coming towards them. Geert gathered the men and they watched in shock and confusion as the trolls descended slowly upon their village, deadly molasses rolling downhill.

"Troldfolk," Mickel whispered. They were familiar with these folk from their native Scandinavia.

"Why are they here?" Hektor asked.

"What do we do?" Geert said.

Dagfin shrugged. "I'd wager we brought them with us. Let's hide. Then we can follow them back to where they sleep and burn them."

"No, no, we can't kill them. It is bad luck to kill a troll," insisted Sigurd, Agnes' husband.

"Ah, that's right. I had nearly forgotten. Then we shall trick them," Dagfin offered, "But tonight, let us scare them off to buy us time to make our plan." He shot off an arrow. The others followed suit and rained arrows on the advancing trolls. They still came, not understanding, until one of them was struck in the leg, an arrowhead embedded in its shin.

"I am hurt," said one.

"Let's turn around," said another. With grunts and groans, they turned slowly and made their way back up the hill, away from the glen.

The men followed the trolls, and watched them turn to stone in the rising sun.

Confident they could outrun the trolls, when the light faded from the sky the next night, the men were there as the trolls animated into living creatures once again. All of the children of the village were with them, sharing a terrified silence.

Dagfin spoke, "Let's make a bargain."

"We do not bargain with humans," one said.

"We only eat them," said another.

"You can have these children, if tonight, instead of eating, you pick up the stones around our village, and bring them back here."

Several of the trolls grunted. "We will only do this if you bring us children every night," one said.

"Then you cannot have all of these in one night, for they are all our children and we will have none left to bring tomorrow night," Dagfin reasoned.

"Bring us three every night," said one.

"No, four," said another.

"Bargain stuck," said Dagfin.

The trolls followed the men to the glen and picked up huge, man-sized rocks as they were directed, balancing them on their heads, and marched them back up the hill, moving even more slowly with the weight of the stones than they would have without them. They reached the top just as the sun was coming over the horizon. Several trolls grunted as their arms grew too heavy to hold over their heads and they dropped them to their sides. Each troll froze in turn, resembling the great stones perched atop their heads.

Dagfin nodded to Mickel, who gave rope to each man present. They scaled the stones that were trolls and climbed on top of the rocks on their heads. The men jumped on the stones yelling, "Die! Die! I crush your skull!"

The trolls groaned inwardly with silent groans, and thinking they had died, never willed themselves to move again. The stones are there to this day, though which are rocks and which are trolls, it is now impossible to say.

Mama's Voice

December 1946

Sometimes when we did our washing
at the lake, scrubbed collars against rocks,
spread linens to whiten in sun, Mama
would talk. Eikil by the River, where
she grew, was haunted by trolls
and *hulder*, and she herded the cows
with an eye over her shoulder.
When she came to Breland as a bride,
it was God's voice that spoke to her.
With each child she bore, the footsteps
of troll and *hulder* sounded farther off,
their grunting and chanting harder to hear.

One day, when we sat among drying clothes,
Mama shivered, leaned into the wind.
She told of *hulder*, those lovely women
who came out of woods and fields to join in
village celebrations. Their voices were
as soft and golden as their unbraided hair.
They waited until midnight to come,
when the ale bowl was empty—
and their strangeness would go unnoticed.
They danced, faster, faster, their skirts full,
their bare feet blurring. Only the watchful
would see under the skirt's widest swing
the tail that hung like a long cow's tail.
A sleepy child or lovestruck man could
vanish, unknowing or knowing too late.
It almost happened to Mama as a girl.
Tante screamed in time when she
spied the tip of that tail brush the floor,

and Mama fled to Nana's warm skirts.
It was longing I heard in Mama's voice.

I hold this letter from Gunnvor in my hand.
Mama's grave must be a lie. I can still hear
the laugh she saved for washing day. She
even took down her hair, let wind lift it
toward sun. In moonlight, or when daylight
comes at a certain angle through the trees
on my soapy hands, I can still almost feel
a tail swinging from the end of my spine.

By Linda Strever

Lock's Half

Patricia S. Bowne

There was once a king named Winter, and he had a magician named Lock, and between them they locked up summer and happiness in a dark cave and left them there. The people hated them, but what could they do? Whoever complained was given to Lock, to disappear into his dark cave forever. Thus men say, 'A thousand locks with but one key.'

Soon enough, everyone interesting in the whole kingdom had been locked up in Lock's dark cave. The only people left outside were like dry leaves, that go with whatever wind that blows and change direction as fast as it bids them.

"We rule a worthless people," Winter said to Lock.

"They are our hands and feet," Lock answered. "Do you ask your hands and feet to amuse you? A kingdom with two heads has heads enough."

King Winter did not like this answer, for two reasons. First, he had begun to think of a wife, and he wanted a wife who would amuse him more than his own hands did. Second, he could not help thinking that for every creature he had seen, one head was enough. And whose head did Lock think was most important, in this kingdom?

Therefore, without ever a word spoken, King Winter and his magician Lock fell out-of-sorts with one another. And each of them began looking to one side and another for allies who would stand behind them more firmly than dry leaves.

At last, King Winter said to his magician, "I must wed and get me an heir. What kingdom shall we ally ourselves with?"

Aha, thought Lock, *you ask me who I would have as enemies?*

"The King of Riksdal," he answered. "His daughter Aniset is the most beautiful girl in ten kingdoms around."

Which she was; and the King of Riksdal was the driest of leaves, wavering with every breeze.

"Well, bring me her picture," said King Winter. "And every other princess you recommend. Let me see pictures of them all."

So he thought to discover all the princesses acceptable to his magician, that he might look elsewhere.

But Magician Lock was more canny than his master, and he brought pictures by the hundred. Surely there was not a woman of lineage in the twenty kingdoms of the world whose likeness did not grace his majesty's walls! And in his magician's bland face King Winter read *All these are mine, it matters not which you choose.* And the King's heart boiled within him, even as he thanked Lock for his efforts.

Now the third day of the third month was near upon them, and King Winter declared that he would go questing, as is the habit of noblemen in Bergheim. Alone he would quest, for three days. "You must be the city's head while I am gone," he said to Magician Lock. "When I return, I will know how to choose a bride."

That morning he rode out of the City's southern gate. But no sooner was he out of sight, than he dismounted from his horse and stripped to his skin;

naked, unarmed, and on foot, he turned onto the path leading north and forded the river in the hills above Bergheim, until he stood in the troll mountains. There he found a stone with three knobs of quartz in it, and struck his hand upon them until it bled, for this is how you summon trolls.

"I am Winter, ruler of all the Riksdal Valley!" he cried, and the echoes answered him; before they had ceased their racket, the ground sprung open and ten troll soldiers stood before him.

"I am King Winter, and I seek a bride," said the King.

The troll soldiers spoke among themselves in the low language, but never a word did they say to the king. They closed ranks around him and into the mountain he went, through tunnels long and low. At last the rock opened around him, darkness gave way to light, and he stood in the presence of the troll King himself.

"I am King Winter," he repeated, "and I seek a bride."

The troll king stood half again as tall as King Winter, and twice as broad. Scars seamed his arms and legs, but his marking-artists had turned them into runes of protection and maps of the mountains. A hundred golden kill-rings decked his ears, and around his neck, he wore twenty soulstones. He looked long at King Winter, pale and naked between the armored trolls, and then he spoke.

"I have no daughters."

"I care not," said King Winter. "We have women and to spare in Bergheim. But I will marry into the great lineage of the North Mountain trolls, if I die to accomplish it."

"How you do so? My sons not have you," said the troll king, and all his warriors laughed like mocking crows.

"I will marry whatever woman my magician, Lock, sends me," said King Winter. "But the soul I marry – that will be a troll soul."

At this, all fell silent. For a long time, the troll king looked at King Winter. Then his hands went to his chest, and he lifted a soulstone, bright and glowing, off over his head. He rolled it between his hands, looking at it lovingly, as far as King Winter could read a troll's face, and then he held it out to the king.

"I lend you soul," he said. "This youngest daughter, not live but an hour. You wed, but not know until six years old. Or I kill. After six years, get me grandchild and we be family."

King Winter liked this little, for it meant six years at least before the troll king would be his ally.

"What if she dies before the six years are finished?"

"Catch soul and bring back," the king said. "Or give another body. But if soul rot in grave, I kill you all."

For there is no worse fate, to a troll, than to have the soul buried with the body. This is why a troll warrior, who comes upon one dying, must catch the last breath in a soulstone, even if it means using the stone he carries to save his own soul in. And if he comes upon a body already cold, he must split its head open with his axe to free the soul even if the delay means his own death. For a man who leaves the soul of another to rot is cursed by the very ground, and stones will eat his whole line, bodies and souls.

King Winter put the soulstone around his neck and felt its glow through his chest into his heart. From that moment, would he or not, he loved the troll princess who had lived but an hour. And the troll king smiled to himself as he watched the king disappear back into the long, dark passageways.

When King Winter returned from his three days' hunting, he had decided on a bride. That is, he had decided that he cared nothing about a bride.

"Choose whoever pleases you, so she be ripe and ready to bear," he told Magician Lock. "For if I die without issue, the land will lose not one head but two."

Magician Lock nodded comfortably. Was this not what he had planned, when he brought the hundred pictures to the King's chambers? He sent to the King of Riksdal, and within a week Princess Aniset was made ready, with her thirty soldiers and her twelve serving-maids, her five white horses and her golden carriage and three wagons of jewels and fine goods for her bride-price, all trot-trotting up the road from Riksdal, until they reached the walls of Bergheim. There King Winter waited for them, with his own twenty knights and ten heralds; so they proceeded to the castle, the people applauding them like so many dry leaves rustling in the wind, and there they were wedded in the sight of gods and men, and what mattered more, in the sight of Magician Lock and the bride's father. Treaties were signed, to no point, for the only treaty the King of Riksdal pleased to abide by was the one in Lock's glances, and the only one King Winter cared for was the one that hung against his breast.

That night, King Winter came to his bride's bed-chamber. Fair she was as summer sun and golden apples, round and fresh, with eyes that sparkled brown and hair that shimmered pale as ash-leaves in autumn.

"Ah, my beautiful love," said King Winter, and caressed her shoulder. "What a treasure your father has brought me," he said, and touched her cheek. "How I will care for you, and you for me," he said, and put his hand on her throat, and there he strangled the girl, she struggling and gasping under his hand, her bright eyes darkened with horror. No sooner had her eyes closed than he took his hand away and laid the shining soulstone on her lips. Aniset gasped and the troll princess' soul, that had ridden on her last breath into the stone, rode out again and into the new Queen's body. She opened her eyes; but now they were round and green and innocent as baby trolls' eyes are. She smiled up at King Winter as she would smile at her father, and reached up to play with the jewels in his beard.

"Sweetling, dost thou know me?" he asked her.

The Queen smiled, but did not speak. Had she not lived less than an hour?

"Ah, my beautiful love," said King Winter. "What a treasure your father has given me. How I will care for you, and you for me!" Then he started up, as one sore alarmed, and rang for the soldiers and his magician.

"Look what has befallen my lovely bride!" he cried. "No sooner did she lie down upon the bed than she cried out that her head pained her; she clawed at her throat, and fell into a swound, and see how she has awakened!"

The King of Riksdal shook in his gold-trimmed boots when he heard the news, for what better pretext for war could there be than a worthless bride? But King Winter laid a warm hand upon his shoulder.

"Whatever has befallen her, I love her still," he said, and any who looked could see its truth in his face. "This sorrow will but give her time, to learn to love me also."

Was it not strange that his magician, Lock, thought the selfsame thing?

* * * *

As the years went by, the new Queen learned again to do the things that children do. She ran and laughed, played and slept, and learned that King Winter and Magician Lock loved her well, each in their own way. With two such friends, what need had she of more? Indeed, she had no more, for the moment she seemed partial to a soldier, or clung her arms too tightly around the neck of a nursery-maid, that person would disappear. Where to, who could say? So, there was nobody around the girl who knew her well, or could note the way she had of starting awake every night, just when she had fallen asleep, with her hand on her neck and a scream choked off in her throat. Nor could any report to King Winter or Magician Lock that at those moments the Queen's eyes were not the green of a baby troll, but the brown of a grown woman. And her face was not smooth and open in those moments, but drawn and filled with anguish. But enough, it matters not. The girl fell back to sleep soon enough, and woke every morning as if new in the world.

One morning, when she was five years old, King Winter played at ball with her in the garden.

"My darling Anna," he said, "A time will come when I will give you all I have, for but one favor."

"What would that be?" asked the Queen.

"Only that you love me best of all men," said the King, and kissed her upon the lips.

"Oh, I already do so!" cried the little Queen.

That evening she walked in the garden with Magician Lock, and they sat upon a bench together. The magician brought out of his pocket a plum, for it was his way to share sweetmeats with the Queen, and with his knife, he divided it in half. Three times he held the plum up and measured with his thumb, that he might divide it exactly in equal pieces, for such was his way.

"You know I love you well, my Queen," he said.

"What is all this talk of loving!" laughed the little Queen. Was it the shadows that darkened her eyes and drew lines along her face, and painted bruises in the hollow of her throat? Magician Lock did not see, for he looked only at his carving.

"The King told me the same, but this morn."

"Did he so? And what else?"

"Why, that he would one day give me all he had, if I would but love him best of all men."

"That's little to ask. Do we not all love him best of all men?"

Who can say what the Queen thought, or how pleased she was?

"So why do you too speak of your love?" she asked the magician.

"Like his highness, I too ask a boon," he said lightly. "To be granted when you have what he has promised you."

"And what would that be?"

"Only to share your fortune, my Queen. Do not forget your servant, in the bright days to come," said Magician Lock, and gave her half the plum.

So wore on every day of the little Queen's fifth year; the King spoke of all, and the magician gave half. What magic was woven into Lock's cake and tarts and fruits, who can tell?

* * * *

One bright morning the sun sparkled on all of Bergheim, and it was six years to the day since King Winter wed his little Queen.

"My darling love," said he to her, "You know you were my bride six years ago this very day?"

"Yes, I suppose," said the Queen, little caring; for she had had no maidservant long enough to tell her about bridehood. To her, marriage meant no more than moving from one home to another.

"That night, you were changed," the King said. "As if you were a slate wiped clean. But look what beauty you have redrawn upon it! Surely there is not a maiden in the land as lovely as yourself. My dear, I would marry you again, for I love you more than life itself."

Again he kissed the little Queen, and she thought nothing of it. Had he not done so every morning, for a year?

"Let us be wed again today," he said to her. "Let our lives begin anew once more, and rule at my side as my one true Queen."

The little Queen wondered at this, for it seemed needless to her; but she had learned to trust and love King Winter, so she did as he bade. Again, she dressed in the wedding gown, and again they spoke words before a priest and her father. And again, King Winter led her to the bed-chamber.

"Ah, my beautiful love," said King Winter, and caressed her shoulder. "What a treasure your father has brought me," he said, and touched her cheek. "How I will care for you, and you for me," he said, and put his hand on her throat.

Up started the Queen, her eyes dark and wide with horror. "No, never!" she cried, and pushed King Winter away with a blow on his breastbone, just where he wore the empty soulstone. Just there, with one blow, she woke the magic her troll father had planted in that stone so many years ago; and it struck King Winter to the heart, so he wavered and fell on his face, dead.

The Queen shook him and called him, trembling, but she found nothing of life about him save the soulstone. Not knowing why, she took it from around his throat and put it upon her own, beneath her gown. She cried out for his soldiers and his magician, but nothing could any of them mend. So King Winter's promise to the little Queen was fulfilled on the very day of their wedding.

Seven days the little Queen mourned, and then Magician Lock came to her where she sat with her father. "My dear Queen," he said, "We grieve with you. But you have mourned long enough, for are you not beloved by all? You know I love you well, my Queen."

Was it the darkness of the hall that turned the Queen's eyes from green to brown, and drew lines upon her face, and painted bruises in the hollow of her throat?

"Say no more, I beg you," she cried.

Magician Lock bowed. "Of course," he said. "Only do not forget your servant." With those words he called upon the magic he had given the little Queen every evening. *Half*, he cast upon her. *Half*.

The Queen started to her feet, and her face was no girl's face but that of a woman, heavy with grief.

"Oh, that you had not spoken!" she cried, tears falling from her eyes. "For now I feel it in my heart, I have no power to do aught but give to you half of what my husband the King gave to me, and what is that but a death?"

She pulled her scarf aside, and all could see the fingermarks clear upon her throat and the soulstone that hung below them.

"The night of our first wedding he strangled me, and set another's soul in my heart, and now must I give half of that death to the servant who loves me best!"

Magician Lock stepped back, but guards had closed behind him. For the King of Riksdal was not loath to give him half a death, and a little more by mistake.

"This is nothing for a woman to do," he said, and put a hand on his daughter's arm. "I, your father, will do you this service."

"And so will I," said a second voice from the door behind the soldiers. There stood the troll King, with his soldiers around him, and how they had come there nobody could say.

"I also am your father, little one. Half a death from each of two fathers is a full death."

But a motion of the hand, from before and behind, and Magician Lock was feathered with arrows, shafted with swords.

But the Queen darted to him, as he fell. "Begone!" she screamed to the two kings. "Never come before me again! You have killed the only one left who loved me."

And she laid the soulstone against Lock's lips, to breathe his last breath into it. She hung the stone about her throat, and never after would she be parted from it, and it was at last laid with her in the grave.

Such was the end of Winter and Lock and the coming of Queen Aniset, who ruled the valley with wisdom and gentleness for all her life long. But when she fell, all fell with her; for both Riksdal and the trolls styled themselves nearest of kin to that lady, and so began the great wars that lasted two hundred years. And even to this day, men say of a bargain urged too fiercely, 'Would you have Lock's half of it?'

A Fisherman's Tale

Laura Lovic-Lindsay

The summer's fishing had not been kind to Brandr. Nor the spring prior to that. Finna herself was hungrier than ever, her swollen belly pushing the table every time she sat. Another child was well on the way. Brandr hoped for a seventh boy and made what sparse offerings he could afford to the gods in that hope. He didn't put much stock in that wish. The gods seemed to have turned their backs on him.

Brandr picked his way up the path between cliffs that lined the waters, careful not to catch his shoe on the thick sea-sprayed mosses that favored these rocks. He trudged the hill homeward, hands empty: nothing to take to market. The other men of the village steered their boats to the far part of the harbor, closer to the marketplace. It was easier this way, their nets straining to contain their haul. Only a short year before, Brandr would have been amongst them, joking and unloading while the youngest boys of the village raced to be the first to help bring the catch ashore.

But these days, he found he was no longer welcome amongst the men; his bad luck might be catching. They became quiet and elbowed one another when he passed. All laughter and joking stopped when he came near: silence, but for wind and water. Instead, village hands busied themselves, stretching forth nets to be repaired before putting out again to sea before the next dawn. The eyes of those too old to fish looked down at their table-work as they cut open the catch, gutting and cleaning, smoking the day's bounty to put by for winter.

Sparse wisps of smoke drifted from the chimney of Brandr's lone cottage in its place upon the cliffs, unlike those too-close homes in the village, clustered and almost huddled together for warmth from the winter winds that would soon begin. The familiar smell of the hearth reached him now, carrying the scent of seaweed soup for yet another night. Their own supply of dried fish had run out in the early part of spring.

He came in as quietly as he could, but the boys saw him and ran to his side, the older ones helping with his coat, the younger ones pleading the dreaded question: "How many fish today, Fadir?"

To this he gave no answer but continued to pull off his boots, rubbing his feet. The older boys, glaring, punched their brothers who dared ask.

Finna squatted at the fire stirring, scooping and handing out bowls. She smiled at Brandr all the way to her eyes, and gave him the largest bowl of steaming broth. He noted every day there was more seaweed and less from their tiny garden. But the coming winter sea could not continue to be generous, even for such fare as seaweed.

Brandr's face greyed over at the thought.

He turned away from Finna that night in bed, ashamed to face her. Turned his face instead toward the wall that sided with the sea. Finna reached over and stroked his hair, kissed the back of his neck. "I will go tomorrow and see wise Ingfrid. She will tell us how to restore your luck."

Brandr was quiet a full minute. His whisper shadowed the greatest reluctance. "You know we cannot pay her."

"She may not want money. She seems to have taken an interest in us. Some of the boys said they had seen her at Market smiling at me. And it was she herself who brought the herbs for the soup tonight. Perhaps not everyone in the village fears the fey that seem to cling to us."

Brandr repeated his concern: "We cannot pay her." He did not wish to be in debt to a witch for any reason.

Finna shrugged, untroubled. "She will pay herself. We will give her half the fish she helps you to bring in!"

The following evening as he walked through the door, Finna caught his eye with a small nod and tight, nervous smile. There was much to do. She sent the boys to collect wood for the night's fire while she whispered to him over the soup, her voice hoarse, drawing with her finger on the table.

Next morning, Brandr awoke much earlier than usual, picked his way carefully to the beach, sliding down sometimes in his haste to begin his morning's work. He readied his boat and made as though to leave in it, but then paused and looked around. Surely it was time.

He walked the strand of the beach, picking up many small rocks, piling them near his boat. The pile grew as an hour passed, then two. He had enough. He began placing them in the sand, almost in full circles around an empty center. Some of these curves he connected with others. Some he left alone, uncompleted.

When Brandr's work was finished, he stood back and thought that what he had created looked rather like the ripples of waves that came forth when a stone was tossed into the sea on a fair-weather day.

Following Ingfrid's careful instructions, he now entered his labyrinth slowly, giving the fey that were plaguing him time to follow. When he reached the center, he paused a moment, then jumped outside the many circles and ran for his waiting boat.

He pushed off, rowing as hard and fast as he could, the sea heavy on his oars. He was hopeful. The fey could not cross or leap the lines of the labyrinth. It might take them hours to work their way out. Brandr rowed until he was so far from shore that the cliffs of home were no longer visible.

* * * *

Brandr walked quickly up the hill to home late that night, laughing sometimes as he slipped on the mosses. It had taken extra time to row toward market and unload, so full was his boat of fish of all kinds. He had stopped in the village to let some of the men buy him drinks. It had taken longer than he had thought. He rejoiced in the many coins in his pocket, the more that were coming.

He had just crested the hill when a figure emerged from his cottage. A few steps closer and he recognized Ingfrid carrying a small wrapped bundle. She turned in his direction, wrapping her shawl tighter around herself. She faced him, defiant, then spun on her heel towards her home beyond the village and walked away.

Brandr stood, watching her for many minutes, then went inside where six boys were already sleeping. He climbed into bed next to the now-empty, weeping Finna, stroked her hair, kissed the back of her neck.

* * * *

Seated before her fire in her own cottage, Ingfrid drew the child near. Few questions would be asked by the people in the village. They remembered well what had happened to those who had dared to question Ingfrid before.

The child slept, sated for now by goat's milk. A seventh son. It had been an easy enough process, leading the fey to Brandr the previous spring.

She felt no pangs of conscience. It was the best possible outcome for all concerned. Who better than she to bring up a seventh son? She would know how best to further his abilities. He would never starve in her cottage. He would know and even play with his brothers. Secrets weren't easily kept in a small village. And as for Brandr and Finna, well it certainly wouldn't be long before they added an eighth, ninth, and tenth child to their home. Ingfrid thought she might even slip Finna some herbs to speed the process along.

The child stirred slightly. She picked him up, holding him in the firelight and began to sing.

The Mara Dream

It came upon me at midnight,
a goblin spirit that mounted my chest
and settled there as if on a saddle.
It grinned

and crushed my rib cage
with lumpy legs,
breathed terror into my lungs
with grotesque bloody lips;
shredding my dreams
with bone-needle teeth,
impregnating them
with darkness and demons,
with crimson horses
and curdling cackles,
and blood-splatter rain.
I rode and screamed

and woke but breath would not come,
and my limbs were stone
and not my own.
It edged closer to my lips

and fed off my fear,
licking and slurping,
giggling and gurgling
with goblin delight,
and left my skin slick
with saliva, clammy
and chilly

from death-nearing fright.
A macabre laugh and it vanished,
as did all dreams of sleep.

In the echo aftermath, I lay there
spent and sweaty, shivering
at the scenes bleeding on my eyelids.
The moon kept me company
until dawn, but even when
the sun warmed my sheets
I was cold.

By Laura Johnson

Young Varkh

Patricia S. Bowne

In the first days of the nation, when we were young and lively and eager and beautiful, the most lively and eager and beautiful of us all was Young Varkh. His eyes shone like sun on the waters, and his yellow hair flowed down like willow branches leaning over the lake to look at themselves. Fair was his face as a summer morn; his teeth were pearls and his body full of the joy of living, like the stallion who rears and trumpets his glory to the mountains.

Ah! With all this beauty, is it any wonder that Young Varkh slew hearts among maidens, whenever they saw him? Truth told, not only hearts did he slay but maidenheads, and left naught but sorrow behind him. Sorrow and hatred, so that as the nation grew from battle into peace, fewer and fewer noble houses welcomed Young Varkh, while more and more noblemen bore him hatred, both for their daughters' tear-stained faces and their swelling waists. In the end, the reward he received from the King, for all that he had spent his youth and vigor freely in the service of the nation, was a holding in the far mountains' edge where there is more magic than cropland, and more trolls than men roam the paths at night.

Young Varkh did not grow bitter under this treatment, however. For his manor was large, and maidservants a'plenty roamed its halls. They were not maids for long. It grew to be a saying in the countryside, when a girl's apron strings grew too tight, that she had "washed Varkh's floors." So are unhappy facts made light of, by those who see no other recourse.

Now in these mountains dwelt a witch, whose face had never been seen. She went veiled from dawn to dusk, and from dusk to dawn no man knows how she went, or in what form, or where. All were sure that she was old, though; for she was tiny and bent, her hands wrinkled and spotted with age and her voice crackled as a campfire. There also lived a charcoal-maker with two daughters, Alsi and Imma. Alsi was the oldest daughter and the loveliest creature on the mountain, unless it was Imma. Fair as morn they were, gentle as fawns, delicate as the new birch-leaves in spring. But for all that, they were poorer than mice. So it came that Imma, the youngest, took service in Young Varkh's household. She went veiled into the kitchens, and never set foot outside the scullery door except to go and come, so how could it be that Young Varkh should hear tell of her and covet her beauty? Ah, none knows the ways of a man's heart, that hunting animal; it sought her out, and stalked her many days, and all befell Imma as it had befallen other maidens in Young Varkh's service.

When Alsi learned what had come to her sister, she grieved in silence. That is the fiercest grieving. She walked the forest paths, rage in her heart and sorrow in her soul, and one day she passed near the witch's hut. The witch called to her.

"Girl! My own heart, why do you rage along the forest paths without me?"

Alsi said nothing, for she was sunk too deep in sorrow.

Again the witch called her. "Girl! My own soul, why do you grieve along the forest paths without me?"

Then Alsi turned and went to her. "I rage and grieve for my sister, who Young Varkh has ruined," she said. "Who will she marry now?"

"She is a charcoal-maker's daughter," said the witch in her cracked voice. "Who would have married her as she was?"

Alsi was filled with fury, and raised her hand to strike the witch. But the old woman caught it in a grip like an iron trap, so that Alsi cried out.

"If you strike the mouth that speaks truth, truth will crawl back in and depart from you," she said. "Now girl, do you want your revenge on Young Varkh or do you want to go your way along the forest paths without me?"

"I want revenge," said Alsi, as if it had never been a question.

"Ah," said the witch, "Do you want it enough to give me your youth and beauty, your bright eyes and flowing hair and sparkling smile? For all these things will I need to accomplish it. If I succeed, they will return to you; but if I fail, they will be gone forever."

Alsi had to think twice, but rage and grief were louder in her heart than fear and caution. She made the bargain with the witch. The witch cut a lock of her hair and rubbed it on her face, her eyelids, and her mouth. Quicker than you could imagine, Alsi began to wither. Her youth and beauty, her hair and eyes and smile all faded in an instant, and she became the very image of the hunched, wrinkled crone that had stood before her. But that crone was no more; the witch put the hair in a bag around her neck, cast off her veil, and stood straight and tall, the most beautiful woman Alsi had ever seen.

"Put this on yourself and wait by my fire," she said, handing Alsi her veil, "and let me go to Young Varkh's house in your clothing. For I think he will soon take notice."

Young Varkh did quickly notice the new maidservant's peerless beauty, and within three days, he set siege to her heart and brought her to his chamber. She was different from the other maids, who had been shy in the face of his glory. Instead, she prowled the room, looking at his little store of treasures; for a man whose vigor has been spent in the service of his country is not rich. "What would you give me?" she laughed, when Varkh put his arms around her.

"My medals," said Varkh, and kissed her neck.

"Those are no use to me," said the girl. "Would you give me your youth and beauty?"

"You have more than enough of those," said Varkh. The scent of her hair was like honey from the fields, and his head swam with desire.

"But if I had need, you would give them to me," laughed the girl.

"Surely I would. When has a man withheld his treasures from a woman in need?"

"And your bright eyes, your pleasant smile, your flowing hair – all these, you would give to a woman in need?"

"I would; provided that woman also gave of her gifts to a man in need," he said. "And I ask less of you, for your gifts will remain with you even after they are given."

So persuaded, the witch let herself be brought to Young Varkh's bed, and much pleasure he had of her. After he had spent himself and fallen into a sound sleep, the witch cut a lock of his hair and rubbed it on his face, his eyelids, and his mouth. Quicker than you could imagine, Varkh began to wither; in his sleep, he became an old man, shriveled and worn. The witch put his hair into a bag around her neck and went her way out of the house, as so many maids had gone before her.

Alsi was sitting by the witch's fire when she saw the woman return, as strong and beautiful as she had ever been. "Did you succeed, then?" she asked.

"I did," the witch said. "Here are your gifts, which you gave to me." She handed Alsi the bag from around her neck, and Alsi felt herself grow young and strong again. She ran her fingers over her smooth skin and strong teeth.

"But what is your payment?" she asked, and then started; for the witch still stood before her young and beautiful.

"I have taken my payment," the witch said, drawing her veil over her face. "Now be on your way, for never will you see me more."

Nobody in the mountains has ever seen the witch again. But many still living had great-great-grandfathers who saw Old Varkh, for he lived there for many years afterward. Strangest of all to tell, he never knew that his beauty had left him; for whenever he looked at himself he saw the man he had once been, and could not explain why maidens' hearts no longer beat hard at the sight of him. Such are the things that befall one who sleeps with witches.

Stranger

October 1948

Papa had a chair, made by his grandfather,
a section of a great log slabbed off for a seat,
the curved back left covered with bark.
Around the edge of the seat was a perfect
row of teeth. Mama said in old times people
pounded into the wood their children's lost
teeth, so the chair would get the toothaches
meant for them. Papa believed it enough
that some of our teeth finished the row.

I wish I could put all my strangeness into a chair.
I'd gather up my hair and bones and teeth,
weave them tightly into a sturdy seat, carve them
carefully into a strong back. I wish I had a chair
to hammer myself into, to complete the circle.

By Linda Strever

Huldufolk

Paul Kater

Kópavogur, early 1940s.

"I'm curious if it's going to work this time," Arinbjörn said as the small group left the building. They'd taken part in a meeting of the Icelandic road commission, debating if the town of Kópavogur needed a new road. The verdict was 'yes' but Arinbjörn remembered what happened four years ago.

"I'm not saying another word about it," Guðbjörg muttered. "I told them my view on it and they laughed at me. I'll be the one sitting at home laughing when they fail."

They talked about the road that should become Álfhólsvegur, or 'Elf Hill's Road.' Not too many years ago the road commission had decided on the very same thing, but back then the road hadn't been built because of 'disturbances,' and finally the project was abandoned when the money ran out. Many people in the area were convinced that the so-called *strange incidents* were caused by the Huldufólk, the hidden people. In Kópavogur, many people were convinced that the elves were present and lived in Álfhól, or 'Elf Hill.' Elves were supposed to be very picky about where they lived and once they chose a location they'd defend it by any means possible. Arinbjörn and Guðbjörg were among the believers of those tales, no matter how hard the reasonable ladies and gentlemen of the road commission laughed.

Work on the new road started only a few weeks later, proving that the meeting had been nothing but a show. The decision to build the new road had been made long before, that much was clear. A heavy truck thundered through the usually quiet village of Kópavogur to deliver equipment, and many men with shovels and carts were recruited to help build the road. Everything went well at first. The debris that remained from the first attempt to build the Álfhólsvegur were moved, and the workers were instructed on how to make the new one.

* * * *

In the Álfhól many had gathered to the calling. Heated discussions flared up everywhere, until the leader of the Elves arrived and waited for everyone to quiet down.

"You have all heard, I think," she then said. "The Mankind People are coming closer and they are going to destroy our home." As was to be expected another chorus of voices rose up around her, so she waited. She did not wait very long.

"Quiet everyone!"

Because of her status as leader she was allowed, able and expected to scream once in a while. Without those traits she'd usually couldn't get a word in, once the other Elves started talking, after such a pronouncement. Of course this was serious, so the others were entitled to some noise.

"And what are we going to do about that?" an older Elf asked, as he scowled from beneath his long, white hair.

"We need to stop them," someone called out, before their leader had a chance to say that they'd have to stop the Big People from wrecking their home.

"Which part of *quiet* don't you understand?" The Elven leader was even louder than before, and this time it had the effect she was after. "Right. We're going to stop them." As if her words were a kind of summoning for battle, loud yells rose up and 'quiet' rang out again in despair.

* * * *

"Why aren't you working?" the inspector asked the group of men who sat idly by the side of the road. He was paid to ask questions like that even when it was obvious that the men could hardly build a new road when there were no materials to build it with.

"Dunno," said one of the men as he puffed away at his cigarette. "Maybe because of the war, or the fact that we have nothing to work with?"

One of his comrades agreed that it was probably the war.

"We need asphalt, boilers, things like that, you know. The stuff that you win a war with."

"The Reich needs all that stuff for their own roads, right?" said another man. The group laughed and then looked up at the inspector again.

"You're not getting paid to sit around here!" he yelled.

"So far we're not getting paid anyway," someone commented, "might as well take it slow on those terms."

In his heart the inspector agreed with the men but he was there to inspect, not to have a heart, so he muttered and growled a while longer and then left the men, assuring them they'd have something to build a road with the next day. The men took that as their cue to head home.

* * * *

Had anyone been present at the construction site that night then they would have been amazed by the view there. Barely visible, tiny people streamed over road, gravel and sand and picked up shovels, hammers and all kinds of other tools that hadn't been put away. Two of the smaller Elves suggested moving a sledgehammer but that proved too much for them, so they resorted to taking a few empty bags. Their leader had told them not to overdo it this first night. "Just take some of their tools. We'll see if they understand then."

After as much had been removed as was Elvenly possible, most of them retreated to Álfhól. Ævar and Ögmundur had been appointed as scouts; they were to stay near the site and keep an eye on what was going on once the Big People came back. Ævar felt proud to have been assigned to such a noble task. Ögmundur wasn't so pleased with it.

"These folk have strange ideas and do all kinds of things that a normal Elf wouldn't even think of," he muttered as they attempted to get comfortable behind a rock. "Just mark my words. They will come and do something unbelievable."

Ævar shrugged. "Let them come," he said as he twirled a stick. "I'll take them on." Daylight came but the expected group of people remained absent. "Ögmundur? Shouldn't they be here by now?"

Ögmundur, who'd fallen asleep, opened an eye. "What? The Big People? I guess so. Why?"

"There are none."

The older Elf sat up and surveyed the area. It was empty.

"Told you. They do strange things. Now they don't come. How strange do you need this to be?"

What the elves didn't know was that they had chosen a Sunday to stake out the site, so the two waited all day in vain and towards the evening they marched back to the Elf Hill to report their observations, which were very few.

Their leader thanked them for their efforts and said she hoped that they'd go out again the next day to see if the Big People would come then. Ögmundur sighed and nodded.

"Do I have to take him again?" he asked as he pointed a thumb at Ævar.

"Yes. He is young and needs to learn. You are old and have authority."

"You heard it. I have authority," Ögmundur repeated to the young Elf.

"And you snore," said the young one. "Maybe that was what kept them away?" He had to run fast after that.

* * * *

"Why aren't you working?" the inspector of road building asked the group of men who sat idly by the side of the road. "There is an asphalt heater now, and two trucks delivered more material."

"Our stuff got stolen. The shovels and hammers and all that, are gone."

The inspector looked over the area. "There's a sledgehammer." Nothing escaped his keen eye.

"Sure, let's put down a new road with a sledgehammer like in the old days," someone said. "I hope you're not in a hurry getting that road done."

Of course they were treated to a lecture on how to take care of their tools after which the inspector paced off, growling under his voice.

"Let's see if we can at least clear some of the stretch," one of the workers suggested. "Lots of rocks there, we can do that at least."

The others agreed. Sitting around like that all day didn't keep them warm and they'd get stiff too, so they rose and began to toss bigger chunks of stone and other obstruction bits and pieces to the side. One of the chunks landed precariously close to the advance observation point that Ævar had selected.

"Oh deary me!" the young Elf exclaimed, "that was close!" He prodded Ögmundur who'd fallen asleep again. "I think we should move back a little." Another piece of stone, landing not quite as close to them, emphasised the urgency of the situation.

"Told you they do strange things," the old Elf with authority said, showing his seniority. "We'll move back."

After finding a spot where no rocks landed, he continued. "And that makes it clear that it wasn't my snoring that kept them away. We'll have to resort to other measures once they've left."

"How do you know they'll leave?"

"They always do."

Time proved him right. The Big People packed up their belongings and left the area. To Ögmundur's satisfaction, not much had been accomplished by them, even when a car had come and delivered a new load of tools for the men. The Elven legion would take care of those again. Together with his young companion, Ögmundur returned to Álfhól where they reported what they'd seen. Their leader was very satisfied and ordered a group to go out and repeat the removal of the tools, but these Elves returned soon. Too soon.

"They put away the tools!"

"Did you do something else instead? We can't have them make progress," the leader said as she frowned. "If we allow them to do what they want, they'll be here in less than two days and destroy our home."

The elves shook their heads. "We didn't know what to do. We need someone with seniority to help us."

The Elven leader nodded, most of those she'd sent were quite young and inexperienced. "I understand. When the next evening comes, Ögmundur will lead you and decide what to do. These Big People have to be stopped," she decreed. And so it would be done.

* * * *

Arinbjörn and Guðbjörg had taken up position not far from where the men were working on the new road. "I'm surprised they're still there," said Guðbjörg. "Last time they did this, the little people had chased them away quite quickly."

She turned to him. "Do you think they've left the area?"

Arinbjörn shook his head. "I doubt that. Elves are very territorial."

"Are they? How do you know? Are you an Elf in disguise?" She grinned at the idea.

"No. It's something I believe to be true, that's all."

Guðbjörg nodded in silence. She didn't want to believe that the Elves had given up on their home. She also wanted to stay to see if the Elves, the Huldufólk, would appear that night. She wanted to know what they'd do. She'd been outside at night before, hoping to see one of them, but they never came where she waited.

"Don't know about you, but I could do with something hot," Arinbjörn said. "We can come back tomorrow, if we don't hear of anything spectacular."

Guðbjörg agreed. They'd been standing in the cold for a while already. Soon it would be dark. Too bad, she thought as they turned to leave. Wouldn't it be wonderful to see actual Elves? For a moment she wondered if she should tell Arinbjörn about that thought, but she decided against it, which was a shame because he was thinking the very same thing.

Darkness and silence returned to the construction area once the work crew had put away their tools and left for home. The place was deserted, but that appearance was only superficial. Under the cover of darkness, a small army of Elves climbed onto the partially-built road and milled about, waiting for Ögmundur with his senior authority to tell them what to do. The older Elf made it onto the road and looked at the asphalt heater.

"We could start with that," he pointed as he walked towards the huge machine. Once near it, he examined the contraption. It didn't look much like anything he knew, but that shouldn't be a problem. "There are some ropes up there, can someone take those off?"

It wasn't difficult for the little folk to climb up and tear off the big wires. Elves had powers and abilities that no Big Person could match.

"Hey, while you're up there, can you see what's beneath that metal thing there?" One of the elves on the ground asked, pointing at a panel.

"No problem. This one?" A screeching sound tore through the night as metal was ripped apart and bent open. The Elf asking wasn't the most patient; even waiting for a yes or no took too long.

"Nothing much that looks like fun," he reported. "Many tiny bits and pieces."

Eager fingers picked out a few parts from the temperature control mechanism and dropped them on the ground. "See? Nothing interesting." Quickly he climbed down again.

Ögmundur the senior was satisfied with the evening' work. "Let's return. A few can stay and see what happens in the morning." He appointed two elves, a younger and a less young one. "Remember, no interfering. Just watch and when you've seen enough you come back to Álfhól."

The Huldufólk didn't have to wait long once the day had started. Soon enough, the scouts came running back, laughing and screaming in victory. Once they had calmed down, they were able to announce that work on the road had not begun as they had clearly damaged the machine enough.

* * * *

"Have you heard?" Guðbjörg chuckled as she sat down at the kitchen table in Arinbjörn's house. "The roadworks have stopped. The Elves were there overnight and damaged an important machine."

"Are you certain? How do you know?" Arinbjörn was curious how his friend was able to learn certain things sooner than the reporters of the local newspaper, and they were always fast because usually there wasn't much local news to report.

"I went there this morning."

"You're a snoop. Too curious for your own good."

Guðbjörg laughed at his reprimand; it wasn't serious, as he said it with a grin. "I'll admit to that, but it helps to know things early!"

"Maybe it weren't Elves," Arinbjörn said. "Perhaps it's someone who doesn't want that road to be built."

"And who might that be then?" she asked. "I wouldn't know anyone who is against the road." She looked at her empty coffee cup. "I wish I knew who did it. Maybe I can go there tonight and keep watch."

"You're crazy, woman." Arinbjörn poured more coffee and pushed the sugar bowl over to her. "Sacrificing your night's rest to sit in the cold and dark, waiting for something from a fairy tale."

"A fairy tale you believe as well." Guðbjörg knew he did. His response, just a glance and a frown, confirmed that knowledge. "You can come with me if you want."

Arinbjörn looked at her in surprise. "You're not only crazy, you're also serious."

"I am."

"And I value my bed."

"But you're as curious as I am." Guðbjörg picked up her coffee, took a sip and frowned. She'd forgotten to add sugar to it. Her sour expression made Arinbjörn laugh.

* * * *

The night was not inviting. Wind threw the falling rain left and right over the raincoats of the man and woman who sat huddled together in the shadows, hidden amongst piles of wet sand. The man muttered something about a warm bed and a mad woman and how he had his priorities all wrong. The woman didn't respond to any of his mutterings. She kept an eye out on the deserted and by now drenched roadway.

"There are Big People there," said Ævar to Ögmundur as he pointed to the shadows.

"I know. They can't see us unless we want them to." Seniority came with experience. "And we don't want them to, understood?"

Ævar pouted. "But it's so much fun to play with them."

"We're not here to play with Big People. We're here to stop them." Ögmundur found it beneath his dignity to hit his younger companion over the head, but Ævar shouldn't push his patience or all dignity would be discarded for a slap.

"Well, maybe later," the smaller of the two Elves sighed. "What are we going to do?"

Yes, seniority came with decision making too. The Elf with authority pointed at a tractor. "That thing has wheels with air-things around it. Start by making holes in the air-things." The zealous group with him charged at the innocent tractor and started making the requested holes while Ögmundur looked for the next victim of this night's endeavour. The rain and wind didn't bother any of the Elves, so when he asked them to break up a small part of the new road, they went at that with enthusiasm. After that was done ,they dragged off the three wheelbarrows that had been left. Ögmundur was satisfied with the night's action.

Ævar beamed as he took in the devastation they had made. "The Big People saw all this happen," he commented as the group headed back to their home.

"I know. They won't talk. Firstly they are older. They know about us, or at least they think they do. And secondly, who would believe them if they tell that they saw Elves at work? They didn't actually *see* us."

During that short conversation the two Big People in their raincoats sat, stunned, wet and cold, unaware that they were subject of Elvish discussion.

"They were here," said Guðbjörg. "We saw what they did. No one will believe us." She recalled how they'd seen holes appear in the tyres of the tractor and how shovels seemed to crawl off on their own accord.

"True. But I owe you an apology. This is something that I would never have seen from my bed." Arinbjörn nodded as he wiped the rain from his face. The rain wasn't impressed and took possession of his face once more. "We should go home now and dry off." His friend agreed, so they rose. Stiffness grabbed at their bones which made them groan, and for the first number of steps they had to lean on each other.

"I am glad you were here to witness this with me," Guðbjörg said as they wandered through the silent, empty streets to her modest house. "It will be our secret. I am curious when they'll stop building."

"The newspaper will let us know." In silence they walked the last few steps. "Thank you again, Guðbjörg. It was a special evening. But there is something I don't understand."

"And that is?"

"I have heard from my grandmother that Elves always know when people like us are near and that they don't show themselves then. Could it be that they weren't aware of us?"

"Maybe. We were hidden well in the shadows and we didn't make any sound."

"Perhaps it was that," Arinbjörn agreed, happy for an explanation. "Sleep well, my friend." He held Guðbjörg's hand for a moment.

"You too. Sleep well." Guðbjörg smiled and then went inside, after which he walked home, his head still filled with amazement about what they'd seen.

* * * *

A few days passed. Guðbjörg did her best not to go and look at the roadworks, although she went around very often to pick up rumours if there were any. To her surprise it was one of the workers who gave her the news she'd been waiting for, when she met him and his wife in the small supermarket at the end of the street.

"Have you heard?" he said, recognising her as the lady who'd been at the construction site a few times. "They're wrapping up the new road. It's impossible to build it."

"Is it really?" Guðbjörg held her face straight as she asked for the reason.

"Someone keeps sabotaging our gear. First a high-powered transformer, then tools, then they took out a tractor and tore up the road, and the list goes on. People got tired of fixing the same fifty metres of road every day, the road commission got tired of paying for that same stretch all the time and so they told us to stop. They're taking away the equipment later today."

Guðbjörg could not bring herself to say that it was a shame; she just wished him good luck and was in a sudden hurry to finish her shopping. There was someone who had to hear the good news.

Winter's White

Cold as ice-death the winds blow in
From over and down the mountains they come.
Why is the wind so cold?
Winter crowds around the houses, beating the walls.
The fires fight for us,
All through the cold dark nights.
Snow is beautiful, beautiful death,
Why does it fall so soft and so white?
Why does evil dress in white?
All winter we wonder, in awe and fear, will we
survive?

By Sasha Kasoff

The Chieftain's Daughter

Kelly Evans

There was once a great chieftain, kind and fair and loved by all, including his daughter; an only child. He was a wise man who lived longer than anyone expected and while there was much mourning when he passed away it surprised no one.

The chieftain's daughter, Ranveig, readied her father's body; for seven days she and her servants prepared for the burial. Cleaning the body, sewing new clothes and gathering the possessions the chieftain had most loved, so that these might be buried along with him to use in the afterlife. On the seventh day, the chieftain was carried from his home to the great grave mound. The men carried their lord, ensuring that his shrouded body was lifted and lowered three times in three different directions. When the chieftain's body was laid in the mound, they placed iron on his chest, a pair of scissors providing protection from any malicious returning spirit. Around him were things of great value: golden goblets and dishes, armbands, torcs and helms, and many swords and daggers decorated with intricate designs in praise of the gods. They placed a shield across his body, before covering him with rocks, soil and sod. When this was done the mourners gathered in the great hall for the sjaund, the feast to honour the dead.

The people gathered around the door of the hall and there awaited Ranveig. When she appeared, two large men of the village lifted her three times above the lintel of the doorframe, as was tradition, for in this way the future could be foretold.

"What did you see?" the villagers asked. They all followed the chieftain's daughter to the Lord's chair at the end of the great hall.

Ranveig had been raised to be sensible, logical and fair. She sat, smoothing her funeral dress as a gold goblet of mead was brought to her. She took a sip before speaking. "I saw a mountain shrouded in mist. The mountain shook and great rocks crashed down the side. Three trees stood and were crushed by a huge boulder rolling down the side of the mountain. After this the vision ended." She took another sip.

There were mutterings in the crowd and one man asked, "But what does it mean?"

The young woman shook her head. "I know not, but this is not the time to discuss it. My father's spirit awaits its feast!"

"And mead!" someone shouted. A great noise went up in the hall and the daughter ordered the food and drink be served. The smell of roast boar filled the hall as a great platter was carried in and over the next few hours all manner of beast and fowl were served, along with more mead and beer.

* * * *

Later in the night one of the servants argued with a man from another valley who had come to pay his respects. "Your lord was great but mine is the greater of the two!" the visitor claimed.

The servant, by now quite drunk and angered by the visitor's insult, roared back, "My lord was much better than yours, you dog! He was a great warrior and as fair a ruler as any man has ever seen! And he had more gold than any man in Iceland, as befitted his station!"

The men continued to argue drunkenly, and barely noticed that three strangers dressed as traders had entered the hall and were secretly listening to the fight.

"My brothers, this is the opportunity that brought us to this valley. Tomorrow at midnight we will go the grave of this chieftain and steal his gold. What need has a dead man of gold? When we are done we will never need to work again."

* * * *

The following night the thieves met by the chieftain's grave, wearing their darkest cloaks so as to remain hidden. Silently they removed the rocks and sod until the gold that had been buried with the lord could be seen through the dirt. Each of the three men had a sack with him and each took enough gold to fill their own sack. They hastily covered the mound, then snuck away with their stolen gold. No one would know they had been there.

* * * *

The next day the chieftain's daughter visited her father's grave and noticed that the turf had been disturbed. Dismissing it as the work of animals, she knelt beside the cairn and spoke to her father of her sorrow at losing him. As she spoke she thought she saw a haze hovering over the mound but she dismissed it, believing it to be an illusion caused by her grief and exhaustion. But when a young bird dropped from the sky onto the grave, cold and dead, this was an omen she could not ignore.

Ranveig announced her suspicions to her household when she returned. "There is a draugr in the village. I tell you this so you might be prepared."

Most of the household listened, preparing charms and offering prayers to the gods for protection, but even the conscientious were not spared the draugr's wrath. One evening a local shepherd was brought before Ranveig in the main hall. His face was grey and he stumbled as he was helped to a stool near the hearth. He gulped down the mead that was brought to him, muttering incoherently, eyes scanning the room wildly. After three cups he came to his senses enough to speak.

"My brother and I were tending our sheep, I went in search of a lamb that had wandered away." The words caught in his throat. "I found the lamb and returned to my brother." The man's hands shook so greatly that the mead spilled over the sides of the clay cup. "When I arrived in his field he . . . they . . ."

Ranveig knelt before the man. "Please, you must tell us what happened."

The shepherd nodded. "The sheep were gone, dead. Their bodies were torn and scattered, some were missing their heads, others had their insides hanging from their stomachs. And my brother, I found him too."

He stopped and took a deep breath. "His arms, they were ripped from his body." The man looked at those who surrounded him in the hall. "As were his legs." He held up his hand and shook his head, unable to continue.

* * * *

The three thieves, who believed they had gotten away with their crime, dismissed the tales of destruction as the delusions of superstitious villagers. They laughed and enjoyed their riches, mocking the dead chieftain though they had been taught as children that this would bring misfortune. One night the eldest of the thieves was stumbling alone along a deserted road. He had been visiting a distant cousin in a nearby valley and they had had much to drink. Singing and giggling to himself, he did not notice that a cold fog had descended on him as he walked, nor did he notice the foul stench that surrounded him. As he neared his own rented lodgings, the cold air had finally sharpened his senses and he became aware of thunderous footsteps following him. Turning, he saw an enormous shape advancing quickly. He tried to get away.

The draugr had taken the form of the dead chieftain but it made a mockery of the man the lord had once been. It wore the chieftain's clothes but the body was so bloated and putrid that the clothes had torn at all the seams and were stained dark with the draugr's excretions. The creature's flesh was dark blue, its eyes glowed white and its weight had grown so dense that the ground shook with every step it took. The thief began to run but he was still drunk and stumbled, falling to the cold ground. He looked up and saw the huge shape was now towering over him, five times the size of any man, it was rocking back and forth, shrieking.

Scrabbling in the dirt and now mindless with fear, the thief screamed in agony as the draugr fell upon him, crushing him so badly that his organs split through his skin. In this way the first thief died.

The second thief, after hearing of his friend's death, decided to return to England. He booked passage on a ship which would sail in three days' time and readied his belongings, including the dead chieftain's gold. The evening before his voyage he made sure a dagger was close, for he now slept with a weapon. He had felt a sense of unease all day and now that the night had come his feeling grew worse. Despite his disquiet, the second thief fell into a deep sleep and was thus unaware of the draugr in his room. The draugr closed its dead white eyes and flew into the thief's dreams, showing the man death and fear and the end of all things. When the thief failed to show at the dock the next day to board the ship, a servant was sent to his rooms, where the criminal was found dead in his bed, a look of terror on his face.

By now the third thief was aware that something was coming after him but was still arrogant and believed that his fellow-conspirators had been weak. He snuck into each of their lodgings and took all of the gold that they had taken from the dead chieftain's grave, storing it along with his own share in the cellar of the house he rented. He barred the doors, covered all of the windows and had a local shaman give him tokens of protection to hang on trees around the property. Nothing would gain entrance to his home, living or dead.

The draugr, seeing what the last thief had done, stood outside the house and in the old tongue roared a curse at the man. Howling as he finished, he flew off into the night. Inside the house the thief shivered in fear but emerged the next morning alive, if a little disoriented. He went down to the river to bathe himself, laughing at his own superstitions and fear. But when he undressed, the smell that suddenly came from his own body nearly overpowered him. Looking down at his arms he saw patches of rotting flesh, pus and corruption. His entire body was covered in sores, some with small wriggling maggots burrowing deep. He ran to the shaman who told him that this was old magic and impossible to cure. In despair the last thief ran back to the house. He had to do something and decided he would cure himself. He heated the dagger that had been by his bed and when the weapon was red hot he sliced the bad flesh from his arm, leg and torso. The pain made the thief cry out and he lost consciousness. When he awoke he saw that the wounds were worse than before and again he tried to cut the infection out with his knife. Again he passed out. The next time he woke he was delirious, the agony excruciating. He thought of his gold and knew he had to survive but there was nothing the thief could do. When they presented his body to the chieftain's daughter he had only a single small wound on his arm. All of the gold that had been taken from her father's grave had also been recovered.

One of Ranveig's advisors spoke. "The draugr has had its justice; it has claimed the lives of the men who stole from it yet it still remains with us. Is there any man in the valley who will help us to secure the creature?"

No one spoke, all were terrified of the beast. The chieftain's daughter stood and addressed the villagers. "I will do it. I will return the draugr to his grave. It was once my father and the responsibility is mine. I require a few men to help me."

The daughter first ordered that her father's grave be opened, that all of the sod and rocks be removed, and that the gold that had been taken by the thieves be restored. She then changed to her warmest clothes and sat waiting by the grave until nightfall. As the light dimmed the haze she had seen her first night at the grave returned and the smell of decay embraced her. She stood and turned. The draugr was before her, enormous, dripping fluid onto the ground.

"I say out loud that I have respect for the draugr before me. The draugr before me is a mighty warrior whom many will sing of. I cower before the great draugr and while I am unworthy to address the draugr, I request the powerful draugr allow me to speak with my deceased father."

The draugr listened to the words of the daughter but was unmoved. It roared and took a step toward her. She gathered her courage and yelled over the noise. "Father! Help me, please!" The draugr stumbled and swayed. "Father, I miss you and think of you every day!" Again the draugr swayed, holding out a decaying arm to steady itself, howling in pain. Ranveig took a step towards the creature and whispered, "Father, I love you." When the draugr stumbled again, the chieftain's daughter rushed at it with an iron knife. Nothing could kill a draugr but the iron would hurt it. The beast fell backwards into the open grave, screaming and grasping at the knife lodged in its chest. Ranveig acted quickly: she jumped into the grave after the draugr and using the same knife she sawed off the thing's head. It was only when she saw the light fade from the pale white eyes that she climbed out and ordered the grave to be refilled.

To this day songs are sung of the chieftain's daughter, of her bravery and of the great love she had for her father.

Prophecy

true or false
no one knows
but all are awaited none the less
dismissed once again
saying they never had a doubt
always worry the second time around
the next unfulfilled prophecy
Danger! Danger!
will there ever be any?
you will have to see for yourself
read the omens
trust your instincts
learn the prophecies
listen to the words of wisdom

By Sasha Kasoff

The Drawer Residence

Margrete Vik Gagama

The first time something inexplicable happened, Torun wrote if off as an odd coincidence. Plus, there was also the cat. But how on the vast, blue earth the cat could have gotten into the closed closet and disorganized her shoes so that precisely each right shoe now stood to the left of its correct match, she could not fathom.

She had started getting things in order. It had been one and a half weeks since she had moved. Her furniture, including the big orange dresser her grandfather had made, the black-and-white long-haired cat Ramona, and herself, had all made the long trip from Lillehammer to Oslo in the moving truck. They now happily resided in a studio on the fourth floor of an all-too-many-of-a-kind apartment building in the city.

Torun's afternoons now consisted of testing odd takeaways, which the small city of Lillehammer could not provide, of unpacking yet another cardboard box of CDs and then running up and down endless flights of stairs to her storage locker in the cellar.

Torun was puzzled. Ramona, the cat, had started eating quite a lot more than usual lately. She filled the cat's bowl with food and water several times a day, yet the cat didn't seem to gain any weight. If anything, the opposite was happening. Ramona stared at her empty bowl, then loathingly at Torun, before briskly walking off to the furthest corner of the apartment, looking any other place than at her mistress. This was odd behavior, even for Ramona.

Coming home from work one day she saw a notice on the announcements board in the hallway. She noticed it mainly because of the capital text and all the exclamation marks. "RETURN the house garden equipment IMMEDIATELY!!!!!!! Axel, the janitor".

Opening her apartment door, she found Ramona impatiently awaiting her dinner. Torun was in a hurry to get her take-away chicken-tikka warmed up and she set the oven to full heat while feeding the cat . . . again. She had missed lunch and by the looks of it, so had the frenzied cat. She returned impatiently to the kitchen when the oven timer rang. She grabbed the oven mitts and extracted a still-cold serving of chicken. But how? She was so sure she had set the oven. Aargh! Torun swore under her breath. Another twenty minutes yet until dinner.

The next morning, leaving the building, Torun noticed a small yellow post-it note glued on top of the janitor's announcement. It simply said "NO! The drawer residence". Torun repressed a giggle. The nerve of some people! Though how strange to refer to yourself as "the drawer residence."

That night she had a dream. She was in her living room when the third drawer of her oversized orange dresser started moving. Slowly, with an occasional squeak, the drawer opened more and more. There was a glimpse of red and a flash of grey, and movement too fast for her eyes to register. She awoke startled. It was only a dream. She gazed sleepily into the living room from behind the curtain that was there to give the impression of a second room when really it was just an alcove. Then she shuddered. Something felt off, but she couldn't put her finger on it. She pulled her bed cover tight and rolled over to the other side. She forced herself to lie still, with eyes closed, until at last, sleep took her.

Torun woke early and enjoyed the way the morning light fell through her window. She felt a bit silly for being scared during the night. Now, in the light of day, nothing felt out of place. She decided it was time to get up and make herself coffee. She rolled over, and there, right next to her on her pillow, lay something unexpected. A red woolen thread. It was wrinkled, as if pulled from a knitted hat or sweater. Torun stared, her forehead creasing in puzzlement. She didn't own anything made with red wool.

That weekend, Torun tip-toed around the apartment. She noticed how the cat's food emptied again. She tried watching the TV, but the remote didn't work. Torun went to get fresh batteries, although she had only recently changed them.

There were no batteries in the cupboard in the hallway, so she skipped down to the supermarket. When she came back, the remote was gone. She looked under the couch, in the bookshelf and all places she could think of. It was so frustrating! She looked in odd places, even though she didn't expect to find it. After half an hour she resigned herself and went back to her couch to read a magazine. And there lay the remote control. Just where she had been sitting. Was she going crazy?

She had to get out, so she went to see a movie. Hours later, when she returned home, she was ambushed in the fourth floor hallway by a sour-looking fellow in dirty work jeans.

"What are you playing at young lady?"

"Excuse me?"

He resolutely pointed at something lying next to her apartment door, and Torun took a step closer to see.

"I told you to deliver it back, now what's your explanation, hey?" the sour face demanded.

"What? I didn't take anything" Torun looked around, confused. The missing garden equipment lay in a heap at her doorstep.

"All right, but I'm watching you!" The janitor grabbed the tools and marched away. Torun let herself into the apartment. What was going on?

The following day, Torun hurried home from work, a nagging worry propelling her to a fast walk. She almost dreaded opening the door, but nothing was out of the ordinary. Torun experimented and made a stir-fry for dinner, while contemplating a presentation she was going to give to her boss the following morning. She had brought her lap-top home and was going to finish the work that night. Just as she started up the lap-top, the doorbell rang.

She opened, to find the sour-faced janitor peering at her.

"Do you have a cat in there?" he demanded.

"Yes, but . . ." she started.

"If that thing shits just one time in the grounds outside, I'll have it taken care of!" he interrupted and added, "I'm watching you!"

He turned and walked away with not as much as a goodbye. Torun felt her heart sink. This was not the way she wanted neighbors, janitors or anyone thinking of her; like she was the lonely cat-woman who didn't give a damn whether the cat littered or not. She sighed.

She didn't know anyone at work yet either. Starting all over was just so tough at times.

Torun wanted to continue working on her presentation. But how odd! She had saved it in "My documents", she was sure of that. But there were no files there. She felt her pulse rise. This was simply not happening! She checked random folders and even "My pictures". She made searches. She looked in all the possible places it could have been. The presentation was gone. She wanted to throw the dammed laptop into the wall, but couldn't. It wasn't even hers. She started crying in frustration. She was going to have to go to work extremely early the next morning.

She decided to just go to bed, so the day would be over as soon as possible. She stormed into the bathroom to get undressed, but didn't look too well where she was going. She stepped on something and felt a stabbing pain in her foot. She let out a small scream and bent to see what she had stepped on. It was a piece of glass. The tumbler she had used for her toothbrush and toothpaste lay broken on her bathroom floor. She had a sharp splinter sticking into her foot and blood had started to drip onto the tiles. This was not funny. It was getting dangerous!

The next night a friend visited. Torun had planned to have a quiet night, but as she grew more and more uneasy, she just had to have some company. Astrid brought a bottle of wine, and as it turned out, Torun had one or two to share herself. Half past one in the morning, Torun finally broke down and confessed to why she so badly wanted her friend to visit.

"There's something wrong here. I feel I'm not alone, you know. And things keep disappearing and turning up again."

"Are you sure you're not just getting a little tired of all the organizing after the move?" suggested Astrid.

"Yesterday, my phone charger turned up inside the medicine closet. This morning, my toothbrush was in the waste bin. That's just mean!" Torun cried.

"Okay," Astrid hesitated. "It sounds like you have some sort of a . . . no, never mind, you'll just laugh," she said and looked away.

"Please, just say it. I'll try anything to sort this out, and if you have a slightest clue, I promise I won't laugh," pleaded Torun. Astrid took another sip of her wine.

"Here's what you're going to try, then. Make a serving of porridge and set it somewhere in the flat during the night. Don't use a steel spoon, or anything with crosses. That's what I heard. I don't know, it's just superstition though."

After Astrid had left, Torun stumbled into the kitchen for some late night cooking. She would try anything, she decided.

The following day was blissfully quiet and nothing out of the ordinary happened.

Another day passed, but that evening, there was no cat.

She ran outside to call for her. Then she saw a bright green and white van in the driveway. "Exterminator & Dog-catcher," said the print on the side. Ouch! Had Ramona been caught? She couldn't have been, she should have been inside the apartment.

Then she saw him. The janitor stood next to the van and jingled a large set of keys. No! He couldn't have!

The possibility of him letting himself in to steal the cat dawned on Torun. He must have set this up.

"Stop! You have my cat," she called to the animal-catcher.

"Ha! You have to prove it! Any cat that doesn't have a name on it can be taken away," laughed the janitor.

Torun felt a chill down her spine. She knew the cat's collar was in the apartment. The dog-catcher snapped his fingers impatiently.

That's when she saw a red woolen hat pop up on the back of the van. She heard small metallic sounds. The kind of noise as if someone was handling the cat cage. Then a dark, small figure was visible in a brief glimpse. Not a person though, it was so little. There was something there! Ramona! She had to save her.

"Please, give me my cat," Torun demanded in a hysterical voice from the animal-catcher. He turned towards the cat cage.

"Oh gosh! This one does have a collar." He opened the truck and handed over the cat. Torun hurried Ramona to safety in her small flat.

"Thank you, thank you, thank you!" Torun was on the verge of crying and petted the cat frantically. "Whatever you are," she felt the urge to add.

That night she made a big bowl of porridge and put it on the floor. Just to be sure. Before falling to sleep, for the first time since moving, she felt at home.

Ode To A Mountain

Oh mountain you are the stubbornness within
Never yielding
You are the home of many a fearsome beast
And the goal of many an adventurous man
Forests cover you like hair
Rivers carve into your skin
Like wrinkles on an old man's face
In the winter you have a dusting of snow
That gradually grows into a blanket of white
Covering you for the long cold months
Till green spring comes to you again
O mountain, what knowledge lies within your
cavernous halls?
What secrets do you hold but cannot say
What rock should I turn to find what it is I seek?
Soft crushed pine needles blanket your floor
Muffle my footsteps as I walk the path up
As I conquer the apex at last
Wind-whipped with exhilaration
I look down upon the world with ceaseless wonder
I feel as though I could float among the clouds
The White Mountains in the sky
Closer than ever before
And still they fly out of my reach
Oh mountain, stand tall
Never stop trying to reach your brothers in the
heavens
Aspire to be better
But never forget
They are but shadows of your glory
Pale as ghosts
As insubstantial and fleeting as a wish

They aspire to be like you
To no longer merely be reflections
Unreal and insubstantial
They are lost in the blue sky above you
At the wind's whim
They have no anchor
Nothing to hold onto but their envy
Do not lose your head in the clouds
Oh mountain, stand tall
A symbol for all who gaze upon you
Be they clouds or a lone weary wonderer
Lead them to the strength within their own heartsOh
mountain you are the stubbornness within
The will to go on within us all

By Sasha Kasoff

Gustave Trolle (1488-1533)
The Gammeltroll of Gamlastan

Mikaela von Kursell

riddle (noun)

1) a mystifying, misleading, or puzzling question posed as a problem to be solved

2) something or someone difficult to understand

(Merriam-Webster)

Present Day

In the beginning, there were three northern brothers: Danmark (Denmark), Norge (Norway), and the youngest brother, Sverige (Sweden). The youngest wanted to get away from the eldest, for the youngest believed there were riches to be had in a life lived apart. And I am the son of the youngest brother, born of his loins, with the same taste for stamped gold, but he rejected me. And the moment he rejected me, forced me to lock myself up in the fortress of Almarestäket, was the moment I rejected him. This marks the beginning of a quick succession of riddles: are ye a traitor if ye were betrayed first?

Gus Eriksson is an old man, perhaps the oldest man in Stockholm, so old and tired he sometimes forgets his parents' names, or his name, or the fact that when he was forty-five, he was once Gustave Eriksson Trolle, the Archbishop of Uppsala, and the first real traitor of Sweden, with the golden-red hair and supercilious blue eyes and the skin so celestial and fine the historians called him the cold white tower and used oil paintings of his own image to support the claim.

And this is the second riddle: what do you call a man who is not a man but looks like a man, who despite his own self-proclaimed innocence, spends all of his free time window shopping and crunching on stones?

Now, he is a *Gammeltroll*, the oldest and largest of all trolls, a hulking figure in black rags. He pushes his hotdog cart, his *korvkiosk*, over the cobbled streets of *Gamla Stan*, the old part of Stockholm, also known as *Staden Mellan Broarna*, the town between the bridges, and the bridges are everywhere, over fifty of them, sprawling in all directions, so many shadows and shades to sit underneath, he sometimes trembles at the thought of it all, even as he moves his cart underneath the meek shade of the awnings and hanging street signs of the golden houses with the medieval frescoes peeling off in flakes. He pushes his trolley to *Stortorget*, the town center, and parks it next to the fountain well with the gargoyle arabesques and the rusted gutters, and as he levels the cart with corner jacks and chock wheels, he looks at all the early morning tourists (*pah— peasants!*) and locals with their shopping bags and high boots, and he overhears the playful Swedish lilting, and he pulls out a sign that says, "Korvmester," hangs it on the side of the cart, and begins his day.

Of course, the town center looked different then, when I anointed the Danish King Christian I (under the solemn oath that he would serve us Swedish nobles well) a debt paid for rescuing me, 'twas just a dirt square with an old chapel really, nothing fancy, but this leads me to the third riddle: who would you serve? The country that birthed you and tossed you off like a strumpet, wet-flanked and reeking of her own frantic gyrations, just for wanting a strong allegiance, or the man who comes in from the north like the prince from on high to save your fortress and set you free?

He has a list of all he serves:

-*Korv* (plain hotdog)

-*Korv* with *räksallad* (hotdog topped with pink shrimp mayonnaise)

-*Korv* with *mos* and *bostongurka* (hot dog with mashed potatoes and pickled onions)

-*Tunnbrödsrulle* (two hot dogs wrapped together in a tortilla with mashed potatoes, shrimp salad, relish, mustard and ketchup)

His cart is filled with plump sausages, frankfurters, German coburgers, alpen wursts, Hungarian kabanoss, a spectrum of rich pork with thin skin, and all manner of accompanying slop, it sometimes makes him sick to watch the people eat them, the juice of the first big bite and then the gush, unaware of their servant's history, the sauce dribbling down their chins, apologies, apologies, and of course they seldom tip.

And so I made a list. A proscription list, on King Christian's coronation day, a list of all of the people who betrayed me, and the charge was blasphemy (yes, my eyes gleamed as I said the word without the faintest hint of a lisp), a right ol' blast fer me, and the good king, on his makeshift throne, condemned all of those illustrious men—councillors, noblemen, city magistrates, archbishops—to a clean beheading or hanging (the square was used as a corral, the townspeople were tucked away with a curfew) and I began with John Vasa (the bell-bright gentleman that kept me locked inside of my own cell with no comforter and not even a soiled rag to wipe the spittle of my mouth with).

He boils the hotdogs one by one.

He was the right hand to the unpalatable regent Sten Sture the Younger, the man who really fed me to the dogs, in all of his hunger,

The blistering water bubbles.

anti-unionist extraordinaire, slandering my name, "Pro-unionist, Dane-lover," stripping me of my title, arranging for a new archbishop, terribly sly,

He waits for the moment just before the hotdog bursts, cooking from the inside out, the innards like a puckered kiss, the skin splitting with a hiss.

he was the last to die, and we piled his body on top of the other bodies, and set them all on fire.

He pierces one with a forked tong, the water dripping from the meat, shakes it once and slides it onto a miniature bun.

They say I died years later and was buried at Schleswig, after the Swedes rose up in the Befrielsekriget, the liberation war, and in some ways they are right—'twas wounded in a battle of Osknebjerg, felt the rust of the spear through the ribs and into the left lung, and saw the face of a young field hand, though he be pretty as a page boy, his eyes peering out of the helmet as right as I see you, could smell the fermented hay on his sleeves, as if he had just tumbled out of the barn with a pitchfork.

He passes the hotdog to an open hand, and paws some loose change. "Tack." (Thank you.)

But before I could even let out a breath, the child pulled his helmet off, and twisted the spear into my chest and lowered his face down to my own, until I could count the pores on his cheeks and taste the awful stench of his breath, and he said, "Do you believe in fairy tales, Gustave Trolle?" (this is the third riddle) "And is a slow-witted man like you, kidnapper of freedom, capable of gut-wrenching guilt? I call you by your true name, Gammeltroll, humongous tottering oaf, and you will wander the earth for one thousand years until no one knows your name, until no one knows you were even born."

(All this, as I was dying, the raspy breath of air-pocketed lungs, inhale and exhale, if I was the villain, why was he the one with the tedious soliloquy, his soft hands illuminating his own margins?) When he tired of his exertions, I stamped my thumb into the ink of my tongue and blessed his forehead, then suggested salacious acts a vigorous boy his age could do with a goat.

A child's voice asks for mayonnaise and mustard.

And lo and behold, I died, puff, went out, expired, with images of frolicking gavle goats in my mind, and their sibilant bleating, and then woke up, as from a dream, buck-naked in a field in Brovallen, stranger to my own arms and legs, which looked just like my old arms and legs, except nude, without the privilege of ruffles and bejewelment, and therefore, entirely unfamiliar. (It was only when I was naked in a field that I wondered if the child soldier was actually much older, and perhaps a sorcerer from Gothenberg, a caster of those dark spells called aspersions). And I don't know if the prophecy became true, if I was really a troll, but in that moment of exhilarating shame, with the wind on my pale chest, and my chest bracing against the pale wind, I knew I had nothing. I was the proverbial Job, scraping myself with a pinecone of a potsherd.

And here is the fourth riddle: what do you when you were a magnanimous elder of the Latinate world, a veritable king blessed by the papal bull himself, and you look at your palms and the dirt in the lines and realize you have nothing?

He shuffles through a basket and passes the child a couple of sticky packets.

So, I was as good as a pilfering Jesuit, collecting alms by any means necessary, eating jammy rowanberries and sleeping underneath brambles and hiding in the forests or behind haystacks by day, and taking to the dirt roads by nights, walking barefoot through the farms of Moklinta and Lindholmen, stealing farmer's gloves and mittens when they paused to put the scythe down (it seemed I had grown stealthy at sneaking), and waiting at the doors of farmhouses, listening at the door for passing footsteps, then tiptoeing in to steal broth or bread or stew, or else, in richer houses, trinkets, and baubles, goblets and candlesticks, and sometimes even horseshoes from the farriers of Marsta. Desperate!— perching up in the upper rafters of a barn like a succubus on a maiden's breast and watching the heave of the blacksmith's hammer (and hearing in each thrust the pounding hooves of a Percheron), the black metal glow, and sneaking down the ladder and plucking them up from the basket the moment they cooled, running my tongue along the unnailed ridges just for the texture of ritual, then selling them half-licked to the black market tinkers and gypsies for a handsome price (a couple of kroners with the face of the new king), their wares tied up in bundles, strung up on sticks, and carried behind them.

"Tack, tack."

Desperate! Until I couldn't handle the torturous degradation anymore, and there were rumors I heard of my past-self's unfortunate contributions to Swedish victory, the way in which I had, in my moment in the center, ignited the most successful of uprisings, now a traitor to Denmark too, and of course there were rumors of troll plundering in all the countryside, one never assumed that a mere man could have stolen so much in such little time (I admit, I was often tempted to hoard the wealth in a nearby cave, to sleep on top of the goblets, and forks, and candlesticks, to contort my body over a misshapen mattress strewn of purloined gifts, the edges digging into my bones, if only because uncomfortable indulgences reminded me of home and I've always found the satin sheen of polished metal on skin stimulating—and this, perhaps is where I developed my scoliotic hunch and my arthritic enjambment, the stuffed pains that ache me when the winter comes).

A man orders a bottle of beer.

And then, as with a prayer, I found a crate of liquors hidden in a well, and I stole a bottle of honey mead, pulling the straw off of it, the kind where you can taste faint hints of propolis from the bees, or is it the larvae-nurturing royal jelly, and you know the exact flowers the poor bumbler had pollinated, white elder flower, virginal corymbs and combs of honeysuckle, aspergillum, a wisp o' water to bless the children. Would you believe I had been a vicar who never touched spirits, who barely tipped the blood of Christ to his lips, whose stomach was as pure as the sacraments? And O, lord, the pleasures I felt, the warmth of the blood and the bones, I couldn't even see the faces of the dead men (Sten Sture with his awfully thin lips and the snivelling ferret face), or if I did, it was a coronation pageantry, fresh roses, united countrymen, three brothers unified in glorious brotherhood, and I could sit on a moss-covered stone with my rags on and feel the connection of sun and moon, the centripetal pull, all in circular balance, and it was like I was never called the betrayer, never capable of counter-betraying, pure and absolved, dissolved like the wafer, the warblers, wheat-eaters, and waxwings calling out from summer evergreens like I was one of them, chirruping, flitting, my own feathered dithering, trilling palaver to the sky,

"Ar du från Danmark?" (Are you from Denmark?)

"Nej—"

the gelatinous pâté of a plucked goose, a song straight from the liver, coxcomb, the bow and the quiver, poetry of a drunken sop—and now: from kvasir to kielbasa!—they say my syllables are slurred like a Danesman's, mulling over a potato as I speak, and I say to hell with them!—If I slur, it is because I was spurned, and all's an effect of the slow-burn of living years and years like that, pilfering, half-naked, forgetting, in a half-haze, relegated to the picketed fringes of uncrossed fields of barley and oats until (stumbling) I found my way back to the center. Stortorget, the town center, and all had changed. Bicycles, and horse-drawn carts, and cars and grey busses, and tall rococo houses where there had been none, and sleek skyscrapers, spires of dark glass (I don't have to tell you what you already know), icicles, architectural musings incarnate that would make a skilled metallurgist in Visby turn green, motorsmog aplomb, a pox for the gills.

"Men din dialekt är inte härifrån." (But your accent isn't from here)

"Nej,"

And I looked dim-witted then, they called me the country bumpkin, or else the homeless man of Stortorget, the one with all the black teeth in his head, awfully moody for a Dane (always calling me a Dane, despite my protestations), until a good Christian man picked me up in front of a gas station, for there I was: drinking from a can of Spendrups Julbeer, stabbing the side with a piece of flint—he gave me a hot bath, hot soup, and a hot dog cart, and brought me to his church in Prästgatan, the din-din-din of bells did not cause me (or my frail heart) to burst aflame, though I must admit I don't much care for sitting in a wooden pew, with the balconies and the king's galleries looking down upon me, and the family crests lined up like legions against the wall, but not my family crest, no, not the golden oval with red headless troll, the one it is rumored my father's father's father killed, in exchange for the coveted drinking horn, what we Trolles wouldn't do in exchange for a drink,

"Nej,"

and then there was the priest at the pulpit with his mangled Latin, his half-baked benediction—I think I was, by now, a bit agnostic, if still nostalgic,

"Nej,"

and soon after (it may have been days or years), the good Christian man died. And when he died, a curious event occurred. I began to see the blood run down the streets, sometimes gurgling out of the gargoyles' mouths or else black trumbas, those waste pipes alongside of the houses, as if it were sewage pumping out of the fly catching urinals. Surely you have heard of the Bloodbath of Stockholm, the way the superstitious claim to see waves of blood splash around street corners and over the cobbled stones every November, the blood of all those men who perished by my word, the crime was blasphemy, snaking between tight alleys like tributaries to the Baltic sea, the night amblers and spiritualists following shadows with flashlights, a jaunt and a jest, a pale chiaroscuro, trompe d'oeil, an outdoor party trick.

"Nej!"

But now I see it every nightfall; and if it does not begin with gargoyles' mouths, it sometimes comes down from heavens, looks like rain, drip drop drip, and I look out from my cart and follow the dribbles down into the dirt cracks between stones, and then I look at everyone's feet, boots, and high heels, and they are all walking in it, and then it falls down in droves and no one notices; they walk into stores, or finish their ice-cream cones, or drink from the coffees, and then when the blood looks like it will rise too high or splash alongside of my trolley, I pull up my sign,

"Korvmester," and close the window, and think about pushing the cart to the warehouse, but I always surprise myself: I move past the windows of speckled blown glass and foiled truffles, and walk towards the river, below one of the many bridges (my favorite is Riddarholmen, where the kings are buried), and I like to sit there underneath the bridge and listen to the cars move up overhead, or the steady clip-clopping of the passing carriage (the coachman is a friend of mine), and feel the drafts flow through the passage and watch the gentle chop of the crimson water, the sun setting low on the horizon, and I hear a small voice say, this, Trolle, this is guilt, this is delicious guilt you can swim in—(guilt for myself, of course, guilt for myself, for it is my own bright blood that passes beneath the purple umbrae of concrete, keeping plastic bags and unlaced boots afloat, for I am the troll that lost his head while looking backwards). And it is a gilded guilt. And I can (and do) sit hunched there for hours, a blanket wrapped around my base, and when a pair of silhouetted lovers stroll down the esplanade and look to me for a scone, I growl, shake my head, wave them off, and tell them I cannot hear them (sometimes, I admit I steal from myself, I eat a hotdog, my pant legs rolled up to my knees, my feet in the stream, the juices dripping down my bearded chin, a lick o' the lip to ye), and because I cannot sleep underneath the bridge, because I cannot stay all night without the danger of an officer's flashlight, I push my cart back to the warehouse and field questions from the keeper about the day's sales, and I take the tunnelbana back home, the dark subway underneath the city, and pondering the riddles of my own damned nation, I prepare for the next day.

Hakon Thorirsson's Tale

Kelly Evans

This is the tale of Hakon Thorirsson, eldest son and heir to Thorir Hjortrsson, son of Hjortr, son of Onundr who defeated the troll king Skerand, who was the son of Ivarr the Grey, son of Folkvar who settled his family here. Hakon's mother was Brynja Agnisdottir, daughter of Agni who was the son of Baldr, known as 'the fair', son of Fenris, son of Gunnarr who was wise, son of Eyvindr who fled the fair-haired tyrant king.

Hakon was a widower, having lost his wife the summer of the Althing from the wasting sickness. His twin sister, Lifa, was his friend and confidant. Lifa was married and awaiting the arrival of her first child. Hakon was out fishing one day when he saw the most beautiful woman bathing naked in a tidal pool in the rocks. Her long hair was darker than a starless night, with eyes to match and a grace that was mesmerising. When he saw her, he felt a sense of need like he had never experienced before, so fierce and sudden was his desire for this woman. As he approached he stumbled on a loose rock and startled her. She turned towards Hakon, who saw alarm in her eyes, yet she made no effort to cover her nakedness. Instead she smoothly moved to the water's edge and dove beneath the waves where Hakon could not follow. He watched the sea and saw nothing but a few bubbles where the woman had disappeared.

Returning home, he found his twin preparing the midday meal. Lifa was staying with Hakon at their parents' farm while her husband was on the mainland, gathering supplies. "Brother, sit and eat, and tell me about your morning."

"Sister, I have the most amazing tale to tell. I discovered a woman, the most beautiful I have ever seen and one I must have love me. She was washing by the water's edge but dove in when she saw me." He described the woman to his sister, who listened intently.

"That is indeed strange, brother. Did you speak with her before she disappeared?"

"Alas no."

"Take care, Hakon, for I fear you have fallen in love with a Selkie, one of the water people. You cannot possess her, no man can, it is unnatural. Even if you were to learn her true name and thus claim her as your wife, no good would come of such a union. Please do not pursue this creature." She begged her brother but, despite his great love for her, Hakon ignored his sister's warning.

Hakon went to the same spot every day, searching for his new love. Each time he encountered her she would pause and look at him, then swiftly dive beneath the sea. After a month of frustration, he came across her once more. This time she was sitting on a rock, looking out over the ocean. Her under-tunic was made of the softest silk, blue as the ocean waves, with the outer cloak a deep green. A fine silver pin in the shape of a turtle fastened her cloak. Hakon approached cautiously, nervous that she would disappear beneath the waves as she had so many times before. But this time she looked directly at him and smiled, moving on the rock to give Hakon space to sit by her. They talked for hours, about the sea and life, and Hakon shared his lunch of dried fish and bread with her, although she only ate the fish. When the sun was finally setting, the woman stood and said she must go.

"Tell me your name!"

The woman smiled shyly. "I cannot."

"But I must know!"

"It is forbidden!" She said this with such ferocity that Hakon was silenced, tears of frustration appearing in his eyes. Taking pity on him, the sea woman took Hakon's hand and said, "You may call me Süt, which means 'sorrow', for sorrow is what I will cause." With a sad smile she gazed at Hakon for a moment then dove back into the ocean. Hakon was silenced and turned to go. When he looked back the woman was gone.

Still ignoring his sister's warnings, for he was a stubborn man, Hakon and the sea woman saw each other every day. Each day Hakon would beg the woman for her true name. And each day she refused.

Hakon decided that he would ask the Lord of the Selkies to help him. Standing on the shore, he called out to the ruler using the ancient tongue. Soon the sea was churning raw and thick sea mist surrounded Hakon. A great wave rose and started towards the land; sitting atop the wave was the Selkie King, taking the form of a man, dressed in black with a white sea-foam cloak. He carried with him a flute made of deep red coral and the smell of the ocean followed him.

"Human, you dare summon me!"

Hakon was fearful of the giant sea creature but his love for Süt caused him to stand his ground. "I would ask a boon of you, in return for this." Hakon reached into his pocket and pulled out an exquisitely-worked silver cuff. It depicted the history of Hakon's family and was the oldest and most valuable item Hakon had to offer. He knew that if it was agreeable to the king, he would be granted that which he most desired.

The king was pleased with the gift. "If it is in my power, I shall grant your favour."

Gathering his courage he took a deep breath and spoke. "I would know the real name of the maiden who calls herself Süt."

Suddenly the waves grew and crashed furiously on the shore, nearly dragging Hakon into the ocean. The sky grew dark and lightning flashed angrily, arguing with the roaring thunder. "Ask another favour, human, for this request I shall not grant."

Hakon was heart-fallen. "But I must have her name! It is the only thing I desire in this world!"

The king's anger grew and Hakon could see changes come upon him. He now had a tail like a seal and it swished angrily up and down in the water, and his eyes grew darker and wider. "Abandon your quest, Hakon Thorirsson. You shall not learn this name. The woman you speak of is my daughter and I will use all my power to protect her from the world of men."

As furious as the seas were at the approach of the king, they were calm now as he slowly sank into the depths, his foam cloak floating all around him as he descended into darkness.

Hakon was almost mad with frustration and longing. How was he ever going to claim this woman as his own? He sat alone on the shore, trying to think of a way to learn her real name. A splashing from the water drew his attention and turning, he saw Süt. Her head and shoulders were visible, and he could see light reflecting off her submerged arms and body. Overjoyed, he approached her but as he drew close, he saw that he was mistaken, that this woman was not his beloved.

"Who are you?"

The woman waved her hand, showering herself with water droplets. "I cannot tell you my name, you know this about my kind. I am the daughter of the Selkie King, sister to the creature you call Süt." She spat out the name, her dark eyes flashing with jealousy, for she hated her sister's beauty and wisdom.

"Where is Süt?"

"She is with our father." The woman floated in the water, watching Hakon intently. "You're the man my sister loves."

"Yes, and I love her in return, more than my own life. I would do anything to make her mine."

The Selkie's lips curled into a sinister smile. This was an opportunity to rid herself of Süt and take her place in their father's heart. "Lean in to me, closer, and I will tell you my sister's true name." Hakon did as the woman said.

When he next saw his love, she was in the same place, waiting for him.

He approached her as he usually did and sat beside her. They talked and laughed and when it was time to retire for the day he stood beside her as he always did and embraced her and declared his love for her.

But instead of releasing her to swim back to the sea depths, he leaned close to her and spoke her name quietly. Suddenly she stood straight and still, her eyes showing great alarm and fear. Then with a wail like a storm wind she slipped to the ground, her senses abandoned.

When she awoke she was at Hakon's farmstead, wrapped in woollen blankets, lying on a large straw mattress. She moaned and Hakon rushed over to her. "My dearest, we can be together now, for always." The sea-maiden looked up at Hakon with sadness, but was determined to live the new life fate had given her.

A few weeks passed and while Süt settled in to live with Hakon and his twin sister Lifa (who continued to warn her brother of the dangers of living with this creature), she yearned for the sea. She would spend as much time as she could on the shore, gazing out over the water and remembering her time there. The more days that passed the more she gazed with regret, for she missed her home.

At first Hakon adored her and would not leave her side. He bought her gifts and would not allow her to lift a hand to help around the farm. But as time passed the novelty began to wear off and he found himself tiring of his new wife and her sorrow. His love turned sour and he grew angry, for how could this woman still not return his feelings? He struggled with his own emotions, for partnered with his growing anger there was still obsession, and hope that one day his wife would love him. But his hope faded with time, and he began to speak to her harshly, mocking and criticizing her feelings and ignoring her pleas to be released.

The Selkie King saw that his daughter was unhappy and vowed to help her. Late one night he came ashore near Hakon's farm and started to play his coral flute. The music was gentle and calm and was heard by Lifa's unborn child, who kicked and rolled with each note. Lifa, woken by the movement of the babe in her belly, also became entranced by the melody and rose from her bed to see where the music came from. She walked from room to room, looking for the source of the song. Finally she left the house to explore outside. A heavy mist covered the area and Lifa, usually familiar with the land surrounding the farm, stumbled as she searched. Finally she heard the music more clearly and stepped towards it into the fog.

The next morning Hakon found his beloved sister's twisted body on the sharp rocks by the edge of the water. Both she and her unborn child were dead, their souls taken by the Selkie King. Hakon knew it was no use, that the king would continue to lure members of his family to the water's edge and beyond. He had to give Süt back to the sea.

He took her hand and led her to the water, whispering her real name once more and granting her freedom. She leapt into the sea and started swimming away from him. As she swam she turned back once more to gaze at Hakon, and his heart broke. He would never see her again, and he would carry the guilt of his sister's death with him for the rest of his life.

We are the Huldrefolket

In the forests we dwell
and from around trees peek
at you 'neath butterfly lashes,
tails twitching with interest
at the curious humans
in our woods.

We are the covered ones,
the secret ones,
the *huldrefolket*.
Sometimes we saunter closer,
forget ourselves with lonely men,
hide our tails, disguise our backs.
We sometimes wish our hearts astray,
and dream of eyes that see beyond our skin,
yearning for a soul to linger with us
and love what lies within.

We are the ladies of the forest.
We help or hinder, at our whim:
a gun that never misses,
a gun that never fails to miss.
Which blessing would you get?
Would you grace us with
smiles or scowls,
courtesy or crudity?
Would you grace us with
simple humanity?

Or would you act as if
you'd consorted with a demon,
wipe away kisses as if
our lips were stained with

toxic berry juice,
pray that God was looking
the other way?
(He already was.)

We would never turn our backs
on you; we can't.
Beneath our tangled hair,
behind our wild, bare, animal shoulders
is a hollow, like an ancient tree.
The skin is rough with bark,
wood scraping over flesh,
and at the base of our spine
sweeps a fox-fur tail.

We are beautiful, so you say;
you've only glimpsed our face.
Yet, if you walked down the wedding aisle
'neath the church roof and saw us
as we are, you'd spit
and scream and curse
in God's name.

What man hides from God,
God hides from man.
Our mother rejected us—
It's fair you would too.

By Laura Johnson

Moonlight

Moonlight dripping
Soaked up by clouds
Infects the world
With the enchantment
Of nights' edges revealed
Coated in burnished silver
Shimmering restless souls
Bright flashing eyes
Smooth curves gleaming
Stroll on tiptoe
Soft laughter
Hearts whispering secrets
Dropping them here and there
Swirling in the leaves
Forgotten, as the moon watches

By Sasha Kasoff

The Edge of Darkness

MJ Kobernus

She was not a child, yet she still liked to play; to hide herself and let the others try to find her. She was going to hide now, in her most secret place amongst the stone teeth in the great beast's mouth. They would not find her there. Only this time it was no game.

She called it the beasts' mouth because the pointed rocks reminded her of the orms that had once slithered in the darkness. They were gone now, all slain. Even the ones in the deep earth, where the darkness became thick and sometimes solid. None of the others knew about the cavern of teeth; it was her sanctuary.

When the fighting became too much and the great bulls slashed and tore at each other, she would go there and sit by the river. Never too close, of course. There was no coming back for her kind if they went into the roiling black. It excited her to sit by the water's edge. It was dangerous. Every time she visited, she would get a little closer.

She stepped lightly, avoiding the slippery rocks, and the soft mud that pulled. In the distance, she could hear the challenging roar of a male. A signal the rutting season had begun. The bulls would seek her, vying with each other to woo her, bringing her treasures from the deep, fighting each other for the right to possess her. She had no interest in them. She would go to her hiding place and wait until the madness was gone from their eyes and they could think again. Some of them, anyway.

Quickly she picked her way through the twisting tunnels, until she came to the passage that led to her secret cavern. Another roar, this time closer. She slipped inside the tunnel and thrust herself into a gap in the rock. The hole was just big enough, and with a grunt, she was through, alone in the vast open space.

There were the great teeth, hanging from the ceiling, reaching down to meet the fangs growing up from the floor. She passed between them, careful not to let them touch her. She did not want to waken the beast in whose mouth she stood. The smell as much as the sound of the rushing water led her to the river, and she settled down, merging with the rocks, sensing as much as seeing the flow of deadly dark beside her.

* * * *

Peter Goodman was a self-confessed adrenaline junky. Since arriving in Norway, he had tried bungee jumping, riding the Olympic bobsled at Hunderfossen, and even ski-jumping, although not on a very big jump, he had to admit. However, this was something else. This was spelunking.

He was nervous, but his excitement far outweighed his fear. There was nothing that could compare with crawling into a cave system, hundreds of meters below ground, and then riding an underground river out into daylight. Then, to top it off, fall twenty meters down a sheer waterfall. Only a handful of people had ever done it, and now he was going to be one of them.

Lars and Terje were waiting for him. They were experienced in the caves, and were his guides. They had anchored a rope to assist in the descent, and they were ready to go. Peter smiled broadly. They stood at the edge of a large hole in the rock. One of them shouted.

"Don't worry, Pete. We've done this route a dozen times."

Terje leapt into the hole while Peter hooked the line to his harness. He slowly walked backwards, playing out the rope between his hands as he descended. Lars tapped his head in warning, and Peter turned his helmet light on. The LED light glowed with a dim, bluish hue.

Once on the cave floor, he looked around. It was bigger than he had expected. His light illuminated the rock for ten meters in every direction. He could see perfectly well, especially when Lars and Terje were looking in the same direction, as then their helmet lights added to the strength of his own. The walls glistened, much of them covered in mosses and lichens. It smelled old, and damp.

"Okay, this is the ante-chamber," said Lars. "We are going to make our way to the main tunnel, and then the main chamber. Then we have to use a series of connection tunnels to get down to the river."

Peter nodded. He had studied the maps they had given him and he was eager to get started. He wanted to see the main chamber, what they called *the Cathedral*; he had a little plan for it. They started out, Lars in the front, then Peter, and finally Terje. They moved slowly but surely, confident in their placement of hands and feet. Peter tried to do everything Lars did, and that worked out well. The passage grew narrow and they hunched over before it widened again, getting higher, and in only fifteen minutes of alternating between standing and crawling, they emerged into the great chamber, the Cathedral.

The three young men stood tall as they emerged from the side passage, raising their heads to the high ceiling, admiring the stalactites, which reached downwards like great stone fingers. Lars and Terje had seen it before, but the orange glow reflecting from the rocks showed them to be just as excited as Peter. Terje nudged the American, and whispered. "Go on then."

Peter nodded. "Okay." He took a deep lungful of air and let loose with a powerful voice, shouting out his name to the eternal stone, "Peter Goodman!"

The sound reverberated in the great chamber, echoing back from millions of years of living rock. It was several minutes before the last whisper died away. Lars slapped him on the back and Peter grinned. He could not stop grinning.

"Alright, Peter," said Lars. "Now you've got that out of your system, you ready for something really fun?"

They all laughed, and Terje took the lead. Peter checked his watch and the built-in compass. They were heading west.

"We're going to free climb down to the river. Just be very careful and do everything we do," said Lars.

"You betcha," Peter replied.

They made their way down a series of interconnected tunnels that had formed when the river cut its way through the mountain. It had changed course several times, and some of the passages meandered, while others were relatively straight. Peter checked his watch. It only took another twenty minutes before they heard the sound of rushing water.

They emerged into a tunnel that branched in a north-easterly direction. The sound of the water was strong now. There was another tunnel, smaller, leading off at a tangent. Lars headed towards the main branch, with Terje following. Peter looked curiously at the smaller tunnel, and his helmet light illuminated something. It glittered. Intrigued, he moved forward, casting his head back and forth, trying to recapture the shiny object. There it was again. He climbed into the small tunnel. There, a glittering rock. He reached, but it was too far.

"Peter, what are you doing? There's nothing in there. It's a dead end."

"Hang on. I saw something."

He squirmed his way forward, inching towards the stone that glittered in the beam of his helmet light. Could it be a diamond? It would be worth a fortune! His fingertips managed to brush the edge of the small rock, when the floor lurched. He gasped, freezing in place. Do not move, he thought. Do not move a muscle.

With the ground stabilised, he carefully inched back towards the main tunnel. Then the floor collapsed and he fell head first into the yawning chasm that formed around him. He did not have time to scream. His helmet light revealed only darkness, and then there was water. Lots of water. He plunged head first into a raging torrent. He tried to shout, but only managed to take water into his lungs. He coughed, coming up for air, and his helmet banged against a low rock, smashing the light, leaving him in darkness absolute. He fought to stay afloat. Far above, there was a glimmer of light and faint cries. Peter struggled against the current, but it was too strong.

* * * *

She could hear a bull somewhere close by. It probably had her scent. No need to worry. It could not get through the hole into the cave of teeth, as the passage was far too small for the big males. She was safe here.

Looking down at the blackness below her something caught her eye. What was that? Something in the water. It floated; arms, a head . . . a child?

Startled into action, she gripped a protruding rock, and leaned out over the river, long arms allowing her to swing far. The floating creature came swiftly, and she almost missed it, just managing to snag it on a claw. She heaved and flung the sodden thing up onto the rocks beside her. She blinked.

What was it? Not a child. At least, not like any child she had seen. She prodded it where its stomach would be, and it was soft, yielding. Puzzled, she lifted the creature's head, and it flopped lazily from side to side. Was it dead?

A sudden retching and the creature spewed water from its mouth. It coughed. She danced back in sudden alarm. What if it was dangerous? Her claws extended instinctively, but just to be safe, she took refuge behind a great tooth.

The creature sat up. "Fuck," it said. "Fuck-fuck-fuck."

She did not know what that meant, but it was clearly distressed, in pain. It kept touching itself. Looking for injuries?

"Oh, you've done it now, Peter."

Why did it keep making those noises? What was it doing here? Where did it come from? She slowly raised herself up, and moved into a position where it would see her. There was no reaction from the creature. Even though she was just one arm's length away, it paid her no heed.

The creature tried to stand, and it wobbled uncertainly on its legs. Of course, it had incredibly short arms, no wonder it was unstable. She watched as the strange intruder extended its arms and walked with extreme care, placing one foot down gently, testing the footing, before lifting the other. She nodded approvingly. It knows about the sinking mud, good. However, it did not seem to be intelligent. It was walking towards the river.

She moved silently and stood before it. She towered over the puny creature. It crept towards her, each hesitant step punctuated by a stream of words. Soon enough, she came to understand them.

"Come on, Peter, you can do it."

Another step, foot finding a flat surface. "Good, Peter. That's good. Keep going."

The little creature veered slightly, and she wondered if it could see her after all. It walked past her, just missing her arm. Then it walked into a hanging tooth, and it stopped. Hands reached out and felt the surface. She blinked in surprise. Wasn't it worried about waking the great orm? They were in its mouth, surely it must know that!

"A stalagmite! Well, this might be good if I had some light. I am in a cave with stalagmites. But it can't be the Cathedral. We were at least twenty meters below that level. So, this must be an undiscovered cavern. Shit."

The words were strange, and she mouthed them silently, getting a feel for where her tongue should be. After a while, she thought she could do it too.

"Why do you make so many sounds?" she said.

The creature spun around, then stepped backwards and fell. It's head thumped hard upon the ground.

"What the fuck? Who is that?"

"What the fuck? Who is that?" She mirrored his voice precisely. She stepped closer and peered intently into the creature's face. It was so small, so smooth. She extended a finger and brushed its cheek. It jerked its head away.

"Who are you?"

She could tell it was frightened. That was not right. It should not be scared. She would look after it. "You do not need to fear. I won't hurt you."

"Who are you?"

The question confused her. Who was she? She was she. Who else could she be?

"I am me," she said.

"Okay, then what are you?"

Ahh . . . this was a question she understood. "Troll."

* * * *

Lars and Terje stood by their pickup truck. Two men and a woman from SARS, the search and rescue unit, approached.

"What happened Lars," said the older of the two men.

Lars shrugged. "He went into a rift. We tried to stop him. He crawled into a dead tunnel and the floor gave out. He fell into the river."

"If he went into the river, then why in hell did he not come out with you two bozos?" said the woman, scowling fiercely.

Terje let out a groan. "We don't know. Maybe his body got caught on something. Maybe he managed to climb out. We tried to go down the rift, but we didn't have the equipment."

"Never mind that. You just let us handle the rescue," said the younger of the two men. The patch on his chest identified him as Olav Helleland. "We know what we're doing."

The older man pointed at them both. "You two are in deep shit. The police are going to need a statement. For the next of kin."

"Come on," said Olav, nodding towards the entrance to the tunnels. "Let's get this over with. The sooner we recover his body, the better."

* * * *

The roaring of the bulls echoed through the tunnels, creating an almost unending cascade of noise. Like a feedback loop, where one stopped, another began. In the cavern of teeth, the young female Troll cocked her head to one side, separating the sounds, calculating. Three. Three bulls had her scent, and one was close.

The tiny creature squatted before her. It was scared. She could smell its fear, rank in the air. "Don't worry. You will be safe, with me."

"What are they?"

"Bulls. Looking for a mate."

"Troll?"

"Yes. Male Trolls. They are not quite sane, right now." She squatted next to the small thing, merging with the rocks. It . . . he? sat facing her, but did not seem to know it.

"But they aren't real, are they? I mean, no one believes in Trolls anymore."

"No one believes? You mean your kind don't. What are you?"

"My name is Peter. Peter Goodman."

She mouthed the words, shaping his name. "You give me your name?" Names conferred power. This little thing had just given her its soul. What was she to make of that?

"Sure. What's your name?"

She hesitated. But what could it harm? It was hardly a threat. It would not be able to hurt her, even if it wanted to. She felt a thrill. She would do it. She would share her most precious secret with this strange little creature.

"I am J'ad."

"Jade. That's a nice name. Like the stone?"

"No, only like me. You, Peter Goodman. Are there more of your kind?"

"What? Yes, of course! And they'll come looking for me."

She was alarmed at this. If others should come down, it might attract more bulls. But they were safe here, the great males could not get inside.

The sound of dragging rock, stone on stone, pierced the resounding echoes of the bulls. Jade stood, alert. Someone was moving stone. They did that for one reason. Sudden fear gripped her. She reached down and picked up the little creature, cradling it in her arm like a newborn.

"There is danger here. We must leave."

The small creature's face was a rictus of fear, and it squirmed in her embrace. She held it tightly. A roar that seemed to come from within the cavern itself propelled her forward. She ran with the swaying motion of her kind, taking long loping strides, covering the vast space in seconds. She was at the other side where she knew a small fissure led to a chamber above. She had never been there, but if she could just dig it out a little, maybe they could both get through.

The sound of rock tearing, being ripped from its roots, was followed instantly by the challenging roar of a bull Troll as it managed to force itself into the cavern, pushing through the narrow passage head first. He was small, little more than a juvenile, but still a bull and therefore dangerous. She put the strange creature down, and it huddled in a ball at her feet, while she frantically pulled and dug at the fissure. Slowly it widened, her razor sharp claws, strong as diamond, cutting through the rock inexorably. It was taking too long. She was not going to make it before the bull was on them. Instinctively she knew it would kill the creature, and try to take her, and neither were prospects she relished. She was failing.

The bull was in the centre of the cavern, sniffing the air, its great snout raised high. It roared again. There was only one thing she could do. She picked up the small thing, and pushed it toward the fissure. It slipped through easily. "You must climb. There is another chamber above. Keep going. I will come for you, if I am able."

Though it trembled, it responded, climbing quickly. Then it stopped. Even though it was clearly blind, it turned back to look to her. "What about you, Jade? What's going to happen to you?"

She was confused. What was it asking? Did it care what happened to her? "Run, little thing. Run, lest the bulls find you. Don't worry about me."

She pushed him gently, propelling him forward, and he started to explore the rocks, feeling with his hands, testing for grip. Soon he was climbing. She turned to face the bull. It was close and it could see her. It bellowed its challenge and charged.

* * * *

Two of the emergency services personnel stood over the rift, their helmets casting solid beams of light into the heavy darkness. Olav hung on the rope far below them, swinging gently. He could not see the walls of the cavern. The river had carved out a great expanse in the stone. He shouted, and looked around, lowering himself carefully. He was in a deep sinkhole, directly above the river, at a point far earlier than the location where Lars and Terje should have led the American tourist.

"Peter, can you hear me?"

He cast about, looking for any sign of the American. There was nothing. If he had gone into the river, then the kid was probably dead. Maybe he had been caught on a rock, held by the current beneath the surface.

"Goodman! Peter Goodman!"

Still nothing. He gave a signal and the others started to pull him up. Then he heard it. Loud, above the din of the river. Something primal. It sounded big and angry, and the hair on the back of his neck prickled, goose bumps forming that owed nothing to the cold. Something roared and was answered immediately by another, less powerful roar.

He signalled again, frantically, and was jerked to the top of the rift. The others grabbed his arms, pulling him through the hole. Impossibly, his head span with stories; things his grandmother had told him when he was a child. It could not be true. They were just fairy tales!

"What the hell was that?" said the woman.

"Fucked if I know," replied Olav. "But I'm not going back to find out."

"Could be the wind," said the older man.

"Yeah, the wind," Olav agreed hastily.

The woman looked at them both as if they were crazy. "What wind?"

* * * *

There are creatures below the earth that glow, creating the smallest light, taking the edge off the darkness. Their bioluminescence is subtle, yet as Peter climbed into the chamber above the cave of teeth, he could almost see. He had learned a truth since he had been underground: there are many kinds of dark and the absence of light was the least of them.

He could still hear the bellowing roar of the creatures below him. The *Trolls*. Was it possible? Could they be real? Maybe the knock to his head had scrambled his brains? But there was no mistaking that something had picked him up as easily as a child's toy. Something immensely powerful and rough-skinned. He shuddered.

Yet it had saved him. Pushed him into a crevasse and induced him to climb, to escape. And now Jade was fighting something in the chamber below. He hoped it got away. As strange and alien as it was, he was grateful to it.

There was a howl and a splash, as if something heavy had fallen into the river. He kept moving, cautiously exploring the terrain. Testing each footfall before putting pressure on it. He moved as if in slow motion, knowing a fall would probably be fatal.

His hand touched water. It was mountain-cold. He put it to his mouth and tasted it. A slight mineral tang, but otherwise perfectly good. Moving closer, he lowered his head, drinking slowly from the rock pool. With fresh water abundantly available, he could probably survive for weeks. Months, if he could locate a food source. Those strange glow worms might be edible. Insects were pure protein after all. They may not give enough light to see by, but they would sure be easy to catch.

"Come on, Peter. Just keep moving. You'll be laughing about this tomorrow."

* * * *

Jade had tricked the bull. Lured him close to the water's edge, then turned and presented her back to him. He charged, thinking her acquiescent, and at the last moment she stepped aside. His face was almost comically surprised as he fell past her, the water taking him, his heavy body, dense as stone, pulling him down instantly. She winced at his final howl. Clearly not worthy. Too stupid for such as she. She needed a thinking Troll, not one so easily outsmarted.

Now the immediate threat was over, she went back to the fissure where the little creature had gone. She could not stop thinking of him. He was so tiny, and soft. Clearly helpless, more so even than a newborn. She could not help wondering how it would feel to be so small and delicate, so fragile. She started to dig, excavating the fissure, making it bigger. Twin roars echoed; the two bulls that had followed the juvenile. They were coming for her.

* * * *

Peter stood perfectly still, his every sense stretched to breaking. Was it his imagination, or was there a tiniest hint of a breeze? He moved cautiously, hands extended. There it was again! Fresh air. It even smelled different. He must be close to a passage that led to a surface opening.

A scrabbling, grinding noise caused him to freeze. Something was coming up the narrow passage he had climbed. At least it was trying to. He could hear grunting, and the unmistakable sound of rough, dry skin being brutalised by stone. He wanted to run, to flee. But there was no sense in that. If it was her, she would find him, and if it was one of the bulls? Don't think about it.

He sat down to wait, calming his heart, which pounded loud in his ears. There was more noise. Rocks falling, being thrown? After a moment, he could hear something else. A rapid panting. A heavy hand laid itself on his shoulder, causing him to start.

"Are you injured? Why do you merge with the rocks? You should flee."

Peter smiled. He had no idea what it looked like, but he was happy it was back. "I was waiting for you, Jade."

He stood, and the creature, the Troll, stepped back. He could almost sense it. Not see it exactly, that wasn't right. But he *knew* where it stood. He knew its massiveness. Slowly he reached out a hand and touched it. He explored its, no, *her* body. If the others were bulls, then she was female. Feeling gently, he explored her torso, her arms. The Troll bent forward to allow him to touch her head and face. It was like touching a rough statue, come alive.

"What are you doing, little thing?"

"I want to see you. Without light, I can only get an idea of what you look like through touch."

"Light? You need light to see? You should have said!"

Instantly there was a shooting pain, burning blue in his retinas and he cried out. A great hand covered a brightly glowing rock, and the light dimmed, illuminating the great fist from within. Tentatively, Peter opened his eyes and looked upon her.

He had expected a horror show. Twisted limbs and tusks. His imagination had supplied him with an endless array of nightmarish images. She was not like that. She was a mountain, smoothed by wind and rain, her limbs long and thick, her mouth wide. Humanoid, but not remotely human.

His breath caught in his throat. "My God."

"Now you have light. Now you see me?"

"Yes."

"Good. I am glad. It makes my heart happy that you see me."

Peter took a shuddering breath. He had not expected to like what he saw, but to his own surprise, he was not at all repelled. His hand reached out and stroked the outline of her powerful jaw, rounding her chin. She smiled, and in a second, she went from a thing of strangeness to one of beauty.

"You are a Troll."

"Yes."

Before he could say anything more, there was an explosive roar and the sound of two bulls clawing at each other in the cavern below. Alarm spiked on Jade's face.

"We must flee. There is great danger here. They will kill you if they catch you."

Peter nodded. "I think there must be a passage leading to the surface. I could feel air moving."

Jade nodded. "Some of the tunnels go up, to the forbidden place. We do not go there."

"But you could help me find a way out?"

"Yes, I think so."

Jade raised her massive head, and sniffed the air. She moved decisively, and Peter followed. The blue gem in her hand still glowed, although less brightly. Peter could see the cavern was long, with smoothly worn sides. He was no expert on the formation of caves, but this did not look natural. The floor looked polished.

"Why is this cavern so different? It has smooth areas, like it has been made this way."

"It was the orms. They were great beasts," she said. Peter had to jog to keep up with her. The Troll girl looked back at him, then continued her quick pace.

"Many of them lived here once. Their bodies wore away the stone."

"Orms?"

"Yes."

Peter shook his head. It seemed there was no end to the things he did not know, or understand.

There was a rending of rock and an occasional grunting word. The bulls were cooperating, communicating. It seemed they had settled their differences and were working together to pull apart the fissure that led to the upper cavern. He ran faster.

* * * *

The SARS team emerged from the mountain the way they had gone in. None of them spoke as they clambered from the cave. A police officer approached them.

"Did you find anything?"

They looked at each other. No one spoke. The police officer fingered his radio. "I've got to report back to HQ. What's the sit-rep?"

Olav placed a restraining hand on his older colleague's arm as he looked as if he was about to speak. "We saw no sign of the tourist. He was most likely drowned in the river." The others nodded, but in all their heads, similar thoughts were occurring. Drowned, or something much, much worse.

The officer shook his head. "Not good. What about those two?" He nodded to where Lars and Terje were sitting dejectedly inside a police cruiser.

"I don't think they're to blame," said Olav. "Caving is inherently dangerous. It could have happened to anyone."

The officer blew out a lungful of air. He had not been looking forward to charging them and was glad they were seemingly not responsible due to negligence.

"What about the American's body? Will it turn up?"

"Somehow, I really doubt it," said Olav.

* * * *

"I have never been here before, but I can sense the forbidden place is near," said Jade. "When you leave the tunnels, you will be safe from the others. They will not follow you outside. I think."

"But what about you?" Peter was alarmed at the thought of them catching her, and God alone knew what.

She stopped to look at him. Her eyes wide in the near dark. "You have said something like that before. Does it bother you, knowing if I am harmed?"

"Yes, of course it does. You have been kind to me, and I don't want anything to happen to you."

"Why?"

For a moment, he was unable to answer. When he did, he surprised himself as much as her. "Because I care what happens to you. Because I care for you."

He could see her mouth working, as if she was trying to get a word out. She settled on a simple smile, then scooped him into her arms, wrapping him in her stone like embrace. He huffed, as the air whooshed from his lungs.

"Easy," he said, breath almost gone.

"Sorry. I'm just not used to . . ."

She let him go, then turned and resumed her quick pace towards the source of the fresh air. At the far end of the cavern, deep rocky voices rumbled in triumph. They had cut through to the upper chamber. They climbed up and announced their challenge. The noise was deafening.

Peter and Jade reached the end of the cavern. The walls rose steeply, but near the top, where ceiling and wall met, there was a large round hole, worn smooth by the countless bodies of the orms as they came and went.

The Troll girl picked Peter up and pushed him towards the hole. He braced himself on the sides and started to work his way up the slanting tube. Jade followed, her body easily fitting within the confines of the tunnel. This worried Peter. If she could easily climb here, then so could the bulls.

Below them came the bellowing grunt from one of the males, the other was sniffing the air. A roar of triumph, then the horrifying sound of the two males fighting again. Their alliance was at an end. The quarry were in sight and only one could make the conquest.

When Peter emerged from the slanting tunnel, he noticed an incredibly pungent smell. It was so strong that at first he did not recognise it. Pine! The smell was from the pine needles. They had emerged into a heavy forest. He blinked in the light. Even though it was near dawn, it was almost blindingly bright compared to the deep underground. Jade emerged seconds later. She stood beside him, her breathing quick, almost ragged. Peter was astonished. She was afraid! He reached out and took her great hand in his, only managing to cling to a finger. Immediately she took a deeper breath.

"They are coming up the tunnel," she said. "They will not give up. You must run. I will try to stop them."

Peter whirled around, dropping her hand. "No! I'm not going to let them hurt you."

"Oh, Peter. What can you do? You are too small. They will squash you."

"Come on. We can get away together."

Her voice conveyed her anguish as much as the look upon her face. "I cannot! This is the forbidden place. Once the eye of Sunna is upon me, I will be undone!"

Peter wanted to argue, but the charging bull that emerged from the tunnel knocked into him and he flew through the air. He landed in a pile of soft dirt, near the base of a tree. Jade slashed at the great beast, but it dodged her attack. She turned, fleeing down the mountainside, and it followed. From the cave mouth, another Troll emerged. Although smaller than the first male, it was still huge. It sniffed the air, looking in the direction the female had gone. Then it caught another scent, and it turned and headed straight for Peter.

* * * *

Outside a local tavern, in a village near the foot of the mountain, the CSN news crew were almost finished with a take. The anchor, a young woman with blonde hair pulled into a ponytail, was talking into a microphone as she faced the camera. In the background, emergency services vehicles illuminated the street in garish splashes of blue and yellow.

"It has been over twenty hours now, and hope is fading fast. With every passing minute, the chances of Peter Goodman being found alive are increasingly remote. A freak accident in the caves of Nordland may have claimed its first victim this day. Our thoughts and prayers are with his family. This is Angela Spellman, with CSN, reporting from northern Norway." She turned to her producer. "Okay, that's a wrap. Let's get out of this place. I need a drink."

The cameraman lowered his camera, as Angela turned off her mic. Then all three spun around at the sound that came rolling off the mountain. The ferocious roar of an animal, answered quickly by another.

"What in hell was that?" said Spellman.

"Dunno," replied her producer. "They got bears here, right?"

"For sure, it was a bear," said the cameraman. "I heard 'em like that in Alaska."

Olav Helleland laughed. He stood to one side, near the rescue truck. He poured the last dregs of his coffee out onto the ground.

"Sure, bear. If bears are made of stone and live in the mountain."

Angela gave him a withering stare. "So, what? It's a Troll, then is it?"

Olav shook his head and walked away.

"Well, whatever it is, we might as well try and get a shot while we're here," Angela said. "It'll be light soon. Let's take the truck up the mountain and maybe we'll get lucky."

* * * *

Peter was winded, but he had sense enough not to move. As he struggled to regain control of his body, the bull Troll came closer, its small, close-set eyes roving, searching for something to rend and tear. It moved away, following in the direction the others had gone, and Peter quietly got to his feet. It was bigger than Jade. Much bigger. And uglier too. This thing looked like it had been hewn from rock and animated.

He heard a roar, and knew it was Jade. He had to save her. He had to *do* something. He set out after the Troll, matching its speed. He was quicker here. The trees so close together slowed the big creatures. Peter knew he could not risk getting near them, but maybe he could distract them, so she could escape.

"Hey! Hey you, you big ugly brute!"

The crashing noise of the Troll rushing through the forest stopped abruptly. A series of grunts punctuated the silence, then the crashing sound resumed. Coming closer. Peter turned and ran back the way he had come. At least, he thought he did. He was confused, and his heart was pounding in his chest like a trip hammer and he was not quite certain which direction he had been going. A bellowing roar sounded and Peter risked a look over his shoulder, expecting to see the Troll right behind him. Nothing. He had managed to lose it. The crashing continued and the Troll passed slightly south of him. Heading for where Peter was sure the road lay. Good. One out of the picture. Just the big Troll left. He set off in pursuit of the bull, and Jade.

* * * *

The news truck ascended the steep hill. It was almost dawn, and the road was getting perceptibly lighter. Angela flipped the passenger side mirror up, having checked her makeup and hair for the umpteenth time that night. It was *so* important to look your best on camera. You never knew when you might get a big story.

"We could set out some food, see if the bears come to it," said her producer.

"I dunno. I'm not really sure if this is a good idea. Bears in the wild is hardly news," she said.

"Maybe we could get them to eat you," the cameraman interjected, while turning the truck's steering wheel into a tight turn.

Angela raised a single finger. "You eat me."

They all laughed. They were still laughing when the smaller of the bull Trolls struck the side of the truck, smashing into it at speed, pushing it onto two wheels. It seemed to hang for a second, then toppled over onto its side, as the Troll slashed at the still spinning tyres, shredding them with its claws.

Angela screamed, although less loud than her producer. They were jammed together, both men crushing her under their weight.

"Get-the-fuck-off-me," she gasped.

The cameraman managed to extricate himself, and he pulled his way into the back of the truck. He emerged again a second later with the camera on his shoulder.

"What was it?" he said, trying to open the driver's side window. Angela punched her producer, prodding him to move faster. He crawled into the back, enabling her to crouch, standing on the door, which had now become the floor. Something had hit them, hard. And it was still attacking the truck.

"Don't open the window. Are you insane!" she screamed.

"No guts, no glory," replied her cameraman. He managed to get the window open, and stuck his head out. There was a tremendous roar, and he ducked back inside, his face blanching.

"What is it," said the producer, trying to get a signal on his mobile phone.

The cameraman shook his head. "I don't . . . I don't know. I . . ."

Whatever it was, it had moved. Through the starred and crazed windshield, they could see it. Huge, dark, hunched over on massive arms, thick like tree trunks. It stood much like a gorilla might, if a gorilla was made from rock and at least three meters high.

It sprang at them, leaping into the air, a fierce howl ripping into their souls. The sun rose then above the mountain, its golden light falling upon the leaping form of the Troll. Instantly the creature was transformed, its body hardening to stone. It crashed into the truck, which span around in a half circle. The impact caused the troll to fracture and break, collapsing in a great white cloud of billowing particles.

Inside the truck, Angela stared out at the mass of rubble strewn on the ground, her face chalky white from the flying dust. She touched her hair instinctively, checking if it was still neatly in place.

* * * *

Peter ran as hard as he could. It was easy to follow the path the Trolls had taken. It looked as if a bulldozer had been driven recklessly through the forest. He could hear Jade's defiant roar as she fought off the unwelcome attentions of her suitor.

He emerged into a clearing in the forest, and there they were. Jade was backed up against a large stone, unable to move further. The bull Troll had its arms spread wide, stopping her from fleeing. Peter stepped forward, picking up a stout stick. He threw it with all his strength at the creature's back. It bounced off; the Troll did not even notice.

Slowly, it raised one massive arm, hand closed into a fist like a boulder, preparing to strike Jade down. Jade stood resolute her claws extended. She looked to Peter, her eyes pleading. *Do something . . .*

The sun had risen and the first light of dawn found them. Peter sprang at the creature's back, and bounced off as if it were made of granite. He lay in the dirt and pine needles, stunned by the impact. The Troll did not move, its arm was still raised in the air, ready to strike. Why didn't it attack?

Then he smiled. The eye of Sunna! They had won. The sun had turned it to stone. He started to laugh, in relief. Then his heart lurched when the meaning of what Jade had said became clear to him.

He scrambled to his feet. Barely daring to breathe, he took a step, then another. The bull Troll's back was so broad it obscured his view of Jade, but he knew in his heart what he would find.

He walked around the great, stone creature, and stared in fascinated awe at the Troll that had saved his life in the caves. She stood there, trembling in the daylight. Her form was severely diminished. She was tiny, fragile, naked, and very human. She turned to face Peter, lifting her face, brushing the loose strands of hair from her eyes.

"I had to make a choice, Peter. I chose you."

The Contributors

Andrew James Murray remains firmly rooted in his childhood town of Manchester, England, with a wife who keeps him grounded and four children who keep him young. He writes poetry and fiction, and was included in the latest Best Of Manchester Poets collection. He can be found writing about anything and nothing over at **cityjackdaw.wordpress.com**

Claire Casey is an archaeologist from Scotland. She has worked on a number of archaeological sites in Ireland, Scotland and England, including a Neolithic site in the Orkney Isles. She is currently working on a young adult trilogy about the Norse gods. For more, see **facebook.com/ClaireCaseyWriter twitter.com/CcaseyWriter**

Evelinn Enoksen was born with a paintbrush in one hand and a pen in the other. She finds inspiration in everything. Author of The Soulsmith, a series of fantasy novels, she has also illustrated numerous books, including this one. Evelinn says there are few things more fun in life than being able to create. **evelinnenoksen.wordpress.com**.

Gregg Chamberlain confesses that he watched too many old cartoons, especially those featuring the Matzoh Brothers, during childhood. Which also explains his off-beat nod towards Tolkien in "Haute Cuisine." With half-a-dozen stories in other venues like the Daily Science Fiction webzine and e-zines such as

Sorcery and the Far Frontier, Gregg tends towards the lighter side of science fiction, fantasy and horror, but there are more serious stories pending publication. He works as a community newspaper reporter in Eastern Ontario, where he and his missus live with their five cats, who allow the humans the run of the house.

Heather Norwood is a writer of philosophy, fiction, and poetry in Southern California. It took her far too long to finish college, but now she is chasing the dream and writing her heart out. Neil Gaiman and her six-year-old son are her heroes. Oxford commas, coffee, and her mom make it all possible.

Kally Jo Surbeck is a multi-award-winning best-selling author of several genres. She has over thirteen books, including participation in several anthologies. A few of her accomplishments are Colorado Author of The Year, the EPPIE (Excellence in electronic publishing) Action category. Kally, at that time, was the first woman to have written and won in said category. She is the winner of the Daphne duMaurier in thriller/suspense. Her poetry was her first writing sale at the tender age of twelve. Her works are in several different anthologies, commemorative additions, and one is even in the Holocaust Museum. **facebook.com/Kally.Surbeck.Owren**

Kelly Evans was born in Canada but spent most of her life in the United Kingdom. She is currently trapped in the life of a Business Consultant and has been writing for as long as she can remember, focusing primarily on historical fiction (with a bit of horror on the side). Her short stories have been published in numerous magazines and E-zines as well as a horror anthology. She is currently editing her third novel, set during the last years of Viking Age England.

Prior to her move to the UK she obtained degrees in both History and English and continued her studies while abroad, focusing on Old Norse, Old English, and the Icelandic Sagas. Returning to Canada five years ago, Kelly brought with her three cats and a teacher; she couldn't bear to leave the cats behind and she's married to the teacher, who would have complained. When not writing, she enjoys reading history books, silversmithing, playing the oboe, and watching really bad horror movies. **www.kellyaevans.com**

Kim Goldberg is a Canadian-based poet, journalist and author of six books. Her poetry collection Ride Backwards on Dragon, about Taoist mysticism and internal alchemy, was a finalist for Canada's Gerald Lampert Award. She is a winner of the Rannu Fund Poetry Prize for Speculative Literature, the Goodwin's Award for Excellence in Alternative Journalism and other distinctions. Her speculative tales have appeared in various magazines and anthologies including Zahir, On Spec, Here Be Monsters, Dark Mountain, Rattle, Tesseracts Eleven, Urban Green Man Anthology and elsewhere.

Kim hopes to visit her ancestral homeland of Denmark someday. But in the meantime, she crafts poems about the tales of family history and folklore that have been passed down to her from her mother. Visit Kim online at Pig Squash Press: **www.PigSquashPress.com**.

Laura Johnson is a Canadian writer and poet from Oakville, Ontario. In 2011, she won a Special Young Poet Award in the Balticon Poetry Contest for her fantasy poem "The Night World." In 2012, she earned the Alfred Poynt Award in Poetry at Western University. Her work has also appeared in Voluted Tales.

Laura Lovic-Lindsay is a graduate of Penn State University. A poet and short story writer from Western Pennsylvania, her poems have won prizes at the prestigious PennWriters Conference in 2014 as well as Writing Success Writers Conferences XXI, XXII, and XXIII. Her short stories have won prizes at WritersWeekly.com, WritersType.com, and the Writing Success Writers Conferences XXI, XXII, XXIII.

Linda Strever's poems are reprinted from Against My Dreams, a collection written in the voice of her grandmother, a Norwegian who immigrated to America in 1913. Strever's poetry credits include Adanna, Beloit Poetry Journal, CALYX Journal, Crab Creek Review, Floating Bridge Review, Nimrod, Spoon River Poetry Review, VoiceCatcher Journal and others. Winner of the Lois Cranston Memorial Poetry Prize, her work has been a finalist for the New Issues Poetry Prize, the Levis Poetry Prize and the Ohio State University Press Award in Poetry. A Pushcart Prize nominee, she has an MFA from Brooklyn College and lives in Olympia, Washington. For more, see LindaStrever.com.

Margrete Vik Gagama is author of "The Drawer Residence." She has previously been published in "Lekt og ulekt" by Marie and Margrete Vik, as well as the anthology "Uglesett" by Uglene, of Mo i Rana. Margrete was born in Trondheim, Norway, and grew up in mountainous Oppdal. A geologist, she lives with her husband and two children in Oslo. She is a heathen, a member of Asatrufellesskapet Bifrost, and finds great inspiration in the Norse mythology and storytelling traditions. Margrete enjoys live roleplaying. She absolutely loves chocolate and sometimes blogs at **www.margisaspargis.blogg.no**.

MJ Kobernus resides in Norway. He is interested in everything; from History, to Languages and Literature and so many things in between. He likes to upcycle, recycle, but ironically, not actually bicycle. He rides a vintage motorcycle though, and loves good Sci-Fi and Fantasy. MJ has edited several books, including this one, and is author of the urban fantasy series, *The Guardian* as well as several YA novels, which he might one day publish.

MJ is also an avid gamer, so you might find him online as part of the SC2 community, where he delights in teaching people half his age why they should respect their elders. His special interest is Metaphysical Fantasy. Ask him about it. Go on, I dare you. Visit him at **www.amazon.com/author/mjkobernus** & **metaphysicalgeometry.blogspot.no**.

Mikaela von Kursell received her MFA in Fiction from Florida Atlantic University, where she served as a Translation Editor for Coastlines Literary Magazine.

Her work has appeared in the Newer York, The Found Poetry Review (online), and The Explicator. Last Spring, her short story, "A Fable Alphabetical: The Life & Times of Robert Cawdrey, Told in His Own Words" was nominated for an AWP Intro Journals Project Award. In her spare time, she enjoys translating Swedish poetry, especially the works of Gunnar Ekelöf.

Patricia S. Bowne: 'Young Varkh' and 'Lock's Half' are folk tales from Patricia S. Bowne's upcoming novel, Fountain Girl. More of Pat's short fiction can be found in magazines like Tales of the Unanticipated, Unsettling Wonder, Lorelei Signal, Rose Red Review, and in Year's Best Fantasy III; for novel-readers, there's the Royal Academy at Osyth series from Double Dragon Press. Links to them all are at her website, **www.raosyth.com**.

Paul Kater was born in the Netherlands in 1960. He quickly developed a feel for books and languages but ended up in the IT business despite that. Books and languages never ceased to fascinate him, so since 2003 he's been actively writing, encouraged by friends on the internet. The internet is the reason why most of his work is in English. Paul currently lives in Cuijk, in the Netherlands. He has 2 cats, who think they are dragons. His work includes the Hilda the Wicked Witch series (13 volumes so far), and several Science Fiction and Steampunk books.

Sarah Lyn Eaton is an author, playwright, genealogical researcher, and ritualist. She has a deep connection to her ancestors, with over 1,750 known names, and is a descendant of the Viking Rollo

Ragnvaldsson, also known as Hrolfr the Ganger. Sarah Lyn grew up along the Erie Canal and currently lives at the confluence of two rivers. She published "Of Roots and Rings" in Elf Love (2010) and "The White Sisters" in What Follows (2014). She keeps a weekly blog about her ancestor and genealogy work at **walkingwithancestors.blogspot.com**. See also **sarahlyn-eaton.blogspot.com.**

Sasha Kasoff is a published poet, fantasy writer, and aspiring teacher. Having recently returned from studying abroad in Ireland, she is currently attending University of the Pacific earning her BA in English. Her poetry can be found in two self-published books as well as in anthologies, magazines, and other literary presses. Look for her on Goodreads.

Steve Klepetar's work has been published in nine countries and has received eight nominations for the Pushcart Prize and five for Best of the Net. Three collections appeared in 2013: Speaking to the Field Mice (Sweatshoppe Publications), Blue Season (with Joseph Lisowski, mgv2>publishing), and My Son Writes a Report on the Warsaw Ghetto (Flutter Press). An e-chapbook, Return of the Bride of Frankenstein, has recently been published as part of the Barometric Pressures series of e-chapbooks by Kind of a Hurricane Press.

Copyright

NORDLAND PUBLISHING

Follow the North Road.

http://nordlandpublishing.com
www.facebook.com/nordlandpublishing
http://nordlandpublishing.tumblr.com/

www.ingramcontent.com/pod-product-compliance
Lightning Source LLC
Chambersburg PA
CBHW031026260626
47153CB00017B/2255